Beautiful
Women

Beautiful
Women

Giuseppe Antonio Borgese

Translated from the Italian
and with a foreword by John Shepley

THE MARLBORO PRESS/NORTHWESTERN
NORTHWESTERN UNIVERSITY PRESS
EVANSTON, ILLINOIS

The Marlboro Press/Northwestern
Northwestern University Press
Evanston, Illinois 60208-4210

Printed in the United States of America

10 9 8 7 6 5 4 3 2 1

ISBN 0-8101-6044-7 (cloth)
ISBN 0-8101-6045-5 (paper)

Library of Congress Cataloging-in-Publication Data

Borgese, Giuseppe Antonio, 1882–1952.
  [Belle. English]
  Beautiful women / Giuseppe Antonio Borgese ; translated from the
Italian by John Shepley.
      p. cm.
  ISBN 0-8101-6044-7 (cloth : alk. paper) — ISBN 0-8101-6045-5
(paper : alk. paper)
  I. Shepley, John. II. Title.
  PQ4807.O75 B413 2001
  853'.912—dc21

                                                   2001000909

The paper used in this publication meets the minimum requirements of
the American National Standard for Information Sciences—Permanence
of Paper for Printed Library Materials, ANSI Z39.48-1984.

Contents

Translator's Foreword

Giuseppe Antonio Borgese is an influential figure in twentieth-century Italian writing, and yet he remains strangely isolated and disregarded. He is remembered in the United States as a distinguished teacher and an anti-Fascist exile in the 1930s, while his reputation in Italy rests primarily on his 1921 novel *Rubè*. It goes without saying that this neglect is undeserved.

Borgese was born in Polizzi Generosa, near Palermo, in 1882. In 1903 he received his degree at the University of Florence, with a doctoral thesis that became the basis for his first book, *Storia della critica romantica in Italia* (*History of Romantic Criticism in Italy*), published two years later. Italy at the time lay under the twin spell—combined, if not necessarily compatible—of Benedetto Croce's aesthetic theories and Gabriele D'Annunzio's poetic ideology, but there was a good deal of dissension in the ranks, and Borgese, as a young journalist and critic, took a vociferous part in these literary skirmishes. He was eventually to repudiate both Croce and D'Annunzio in favor of his own reflective approach to literature and life, as expressed in a three-volume collection of critical essays, *La vita e il libro* (*Life and Books*), published from 1910 to 1913. Meanwhile, he was teaching aesthetics and German literature at the universities in Turin, Rome, and Milan. With Italy on the brink of the First World War, he seems to have been a fervent interventionist; it was the sad outcome of such enthusiasm that produced his memorable novel *Rubè*.

Life in Italy under Fascism was intolerable to Borgese, and he went into exile in 1931, having refused to sign a loyalty oath to the regime. In the United States he taught at Smith College and the University of Chicago and wrote, in English, an impassioned attack on Mussolini, *Goliath: The March of Fascism,* published in 1937. (It would be translated and published in Italy in 1946.) He married his second wife, Thomas Mann's daughter Elisabeth. In 1947 he returned to Italy and resumed his teaching post at the University of Milan. He died in Fiesole in 1952.

Oddly enough, Borgese's career as a writer of fiction was confined to the decade of the 1920s. Though he wrote other novels and plays, which have been largely forgotten, *Rubè* is unique both for its success at the time and for the position it has come to occupy in Italian literature between the two wars, and if it too is seldom read these days, it still holds a secure place in the development of the Italian novel. Critics have placed it on a shelf alongside Alberto Moravia's *Gli indifferenti* (*The Time of Indifference*) and Italo Svevo's *La coscienza di Zeno* (*The Confessions of Zeno*) and have been content to leave it there. Yet it is hardly possible to consider Borgese's short fiction without casting at least a glance at this long, brooding novel, if only because it is so different in method, scope, and tone.

Filippo Rubè is an ambitious young lawyer from the South of Italy who comes to Rome, enlists in the army, is wounded in the war, gets posted to Paris as a military attaché, and at war's end returns to Italy, where he tries to find his place in a postwar climate of political instability and economic greed. Although he does his best to act in good faith, Rubè *manca qualcosa,* as Italians would say: he lacks something. This something is what existentialists would call "authenticity." There is an aura of the superfluous man of nineteenth-century Russian fiction about him. In other words, Rubè is a young man on the make whose weak scruples are enough to keep him from making it. Once he has perceived the war's pointlessness, his fear, which is genuine, is transmuted into a kind of reckless bravado that serves only to mask his basic insecurity. As the author remarks: "His having hoped too much and suffered too much from trifles had made him insensitive when it came to truly large matters." He marries the high-minded Eugenia, whose beauty "had no odor of joy, it was as startling as a premonition of mourning," but he abandons her for the femme fatale Celestina, whom he had met in Paris. When Celestina is drowned in a boating accident on Lago Maggiore, Rubè is arrested and held on suspicion of murder, and though he is later released, the lesson is spelled out: "Prison was in some way the equivalent of what at other times he had hoped military service and the war would be: an exemption by higher authority from the need to make decisions in daily life, a social solution to problems that the individual is unable to face." Like Italy itself, he is ripe for Fascism. In the end he is caught up by chance in a street demonstration in Bologna and trampled to death by the horses of the mounted police.

It is in this symbolic vein that *Rubè* has been interpreted by critics, who commend Borgese for his political prescience and then unfairly dismiss him as an artist. Clearly one would need a different set of criteria for the stories gathered under the rubric *Beautiful Women,* where large political and social issues, all the historical factors that count so heavily in *Rubè,* are scarcely touched upon. These are stories of love, and generally of loss, but they are not analytical in the way that the novel is and do not extend beyond themselves. They are vignettes, snapshots if you like, brief and forthright, occasionally enigmatic, and for all their wealth of descriptive detail, they are often vague about times and places. They cannot be said to expose the fabric of Italian society, only some of its more colorful threads. Still, one might mention the range and variety of the female subjects, in contrast to the rigidly schematic juxtaposition of the two women in Rubè's life.

To what extent Borgese's tongue was in his cheek in calling his thematic collection *Beautiful Women* (its Italian title is *Le belle,* "the beauties") would be hard to say, since beauty here remains in the eye of the male beholder. The women do not speak for themselves. Nor, of course, are they always beautiful in spirit, and a few—the unseen wife in "The Good Lady," the mad sister in "Eureka," the American tourist in "The Boy"—are decidedly unlovely. But Borgese, absorbed by his infinite curiosity and fond patience, is harsh only on the men with whom they are involved.

In the story "Lean Harvest," the narrator watches his two friends walk away, and, "as happens in mountain meadows, especially in the September sunlight, the farther away they went, the bigger they looked." This is in preparation for the vision at the end: "A woman dressed in black was wielding a scythe, and she looked too big." (This phantom woman is the Comare Secca—the Grim Reaper, we would have to say in English, ignoring the change of gender.) But death for the moment is beside the point. It is the receding figure of Borgese himself who, in the sunlit meadows of these stories, grows ever larger—and that is not an illusion.

J.S.

Beautiful
Women

The Woman from Syracuse

In Megara they still grow carnations on the balconies, and the women wear long skirts; so when an ankle is glimpsed, you literally see young men tremble. But this seldom happens, for the women walk cautiously and are chaperoned, or they chaperon themselves; and if it rains, they would rather go home with the hems of their skirts muddied than have their stockings devoured by looks as warm as kisses. Anyway, you don't see many women on the streets, except for servant girls and those from the lower classes who still go to the fountain with water jugs on their heads.

Yes, this still exists; the steep little cobblestone streets, from the Marina to the Castello, still exist, so narrow that the women would be overwhelmed, crushed by the throng of men (and so they stay home), so precipitous that people going up on one side seem to benefit by the weight of those going down on the other, like the two sections of a funicular. And always a crowd, as though it were always market day; a dark crowd, dressed in dark clothes even on the dog days of August—but the streets are narrow and the houses tall, their facades often overhanging and shored up, and they don't admit the sun. People walk slowly but res- olutely, their footsteps resounding on the pavement; here and there a group will collect, like flies on the rim of a cup, slowing passage still more; voices are excited or mysterious; greetings from one side of the street to the other are as loud as challenges.

I remember the boom of the big wooden doors as they opened and closed; I remember the bells on the goats as they were driven down in the morning, encumbered by their swollen udders and rubbing their horns against the knees of the passersby. I can still even hear the explosion of Mastro Angelo's sulfur match when he came home late to his house across the street from us and lit his last cigar.

Toward evening, halfway along the Strada Lunga, the smell of rotting fish clashes with the aroma of orange blossoms, thin, acidulous, close to that of lily of the valley; the breeze from the sea is cut short by the dust brought by the sirocco from the Terre Rosse—red as a lion's mane—whose vineyards produce a fiery wine.

Then the women of the lower classes come to peer out the doors at street level, opening their eyes as though they were just waking up. They raise their eye- lids like shutters over their sorrowful and listless eyes, full of obscurity and yellow heat, of indecipherable dreams like those of animals; if someone calls them from inside, they answer, bending their necks, with a whining tone in their voices. Up above, the balcony doors open and the ladies appear; they greet one another and chat, monotonously, incessantly, from one balcony to the next. But should they lean their elbows on the railings, they hold their bodies back; should they sit down, before all else they adjust their skirts over their high-button shoes, for fear that passersby in the street may look upward. Those on balconies with curved railings must take particular care; no one ever absent-mindedly places her foot on the metal.

That is the hour when the women of Megara come to life, between sunset and evening, like morning glories blossoming at dusk.

Then night falls. Lullabies in the street-level dwellings, or quarrels; but the woman's voice is soon suppressed, and after a while the man too is silent. Nothing is heard from the houses of the gentlefolk because they have thick walls like prisons.

I was born in those parts; not actually in Megara but farther up, in a village three miles from the Castello. My family was from Syracuse, but my father had gone away and a short time later settled in Megara while I was still a child.

It had been years since I'd set foot in the place! But then Galliani wanted to go there to do research on the Sicilian quattrocento, and on a whim I decided to go along. But once he was there, he fell in love with the seicento, with its monasteries formidable as fortresses and its churches dripping with music and gold, where the statues of the saints seem about to take flight.

I can't say how it happened; without knowing where I was going, almost unwillingly, I turned the corner, my friend beside me, from the Strada Lunga onto a side street, wide and deserted but ending after a hundred paces in sloping gardens. It was a June day that showed no signs of ending. Down below, a dark strip of sea.

Here I retraced my footsteps as a boy along the high mysterious wall of an orchard, before me a curious facade, between yellow and orange, its single balcony with its black iron railing bulging inordinately as though it had throbbed for centuries to the sound of secret serenades.

"That," I said with a shudder, "is my Aunt Clementina's balcony, the woman from Syracuse."

And I leaned on my friend for support.

For as long as I can remember it was called the balcony of the woman from Syracuse.

She was my father's sister, and everyone called her the woman from Syracuse. You'd think she had come from ever so far away, while actually it was only three hours by sea from her city to Megara. She came to marry my father's business partner, Nicola Laudìsi.

He was a huge, corpulent man, with arms round as Indian clubs, which he had to hold away from his chest, and wrists as shiny and fleshy as those of a gigantic newborn baby. When he took his siesta he kept his hands on his stomach. That was how I saw him a couple of times, and it scared me. He looked like an ogre. He was so tall that you might have needed a footstool in order to touch his face. His mustache, already gray, was barely apparent on his fat and tired face. He wheezed asthmatically, like a bellows.

Being rich, he wanted children to whom he could leave his property, and that was why he was on the lookout for a wife. And so they brought him Aunt Clementina.

She arrived in Megara no longer in her first youth, but she was still far from thirty. She came from a household of orphans, and she was silent.

I loved her, of course, before knowing what love was. Almost every day I managed to be there in front of her balcony at the hour when the woman from Syracuse appeared on it like a queen. But there was no crowd in the street below to whom she might show herself—only myself. Nor were there even other balconies, alongside or facing hers, with other women to talk to, as all the women of Megara were doing at that hour. All she saw were gardens and a strip of sea.

She had no children. I heard whispers about some kind of illness. She often suffered from headaches, which made her look pale as a sleepwalker.

Naturally she paid no attention to me. To get her to notice me, I would climb up the smooth wall of the orchard to show off how daring I was. Sometimes, fearing I would hurt myself, she would call out— "Alberto!"—and it was the sound of her voice that hurt me. So I climbed down and walked over to her house. Aunt Clementina drew back from the railing, arranging her skirt over her high-button shoes.

I doubt that I've ever seen such a beautiful woman since. All you saw of her was her face. The women of that time were not like the ones today, who seem like fruit exposed amid foliage. They went about hidden in a maze of laces and frills, with white starched petticoats, similar to the stiff, fancy paper once used to wrap bouquets of flowers, and over the petticoats full flowered skirts, all ruffles and furbelows, majestic as pagodas, and at the bosom the reinforced, invincible stays.

But from her fingers and wrists, you could see she was thin and submissive, of an amber complexion. She wore no other scent but lavender and that of the Macassar oil that she used on her black hair.

And her face was incomparable—her straight nose, her pure lips, her eyes, though now I wouldn't be able to say whether they were a quiet blue or gray as ashes over a hidden fire.

At the first breath of evening she went back inside. The shadows of the night were transparent, like a shell in which the light of dawn already trembled. Sometimes, on summer nights, a white cactus flower opened, and the intoxicating fragrance overflowed like liquid.

But when I returned to Megara and retraced my steps along the orchard wall, there were no more carnation plants or cactus spines on Aunt Clementina's balcony. The iron rings to which the flowerpots were once fastened were as twisted as old daggers, red with rust that looked like dried blood.

I saw her for the last time one Sunday morning at the hour when mass is sung. She lay dead on the street, covered to her feet by her beautiful white satin dress embroidered with clusters of pink flowers. No longer could you hear the bells of the goats on the Strada Lunga; all you heard—without letup—was the bell for mass.

I was the first to see her there. Every Sunday morning I stationed myself in front of her doorway to watch her emerge. When she came forth for mass—and it wasn't easy to see her in the street at other times during the week—it was as though an invisible canopy were suspended above her head.

I struggled to find my voice at the bottom of my chest and yelled. Her husband came down, followed by the servant woman Zulicchia; a minute later, I don't know how, my mother came running from the other street. We stood there beside the dead woman. She had thrown herself headlong from the balcony.

Later, much later—when Nicola Laudìsi died of an aneurism—I learned more about it. The day before, Aunt Clementina, opening a door, had caught her husband fondling the servant. "Zulicchia" is just another form of "Vincenzina," but I, who was thirteen and had read Byron in translation, thought of her as "Zuleika." She was another beautiful woman, with an odd resemblance to her mistress, except that her nose was too thin and pointed, which gave her a mean look. I always remember the way she would set the water jug down beside the fountain and stand up again; the rolled-up cloth she wore around her head to support the weight of the jug was like a kind of turreted crown above her lovely servile face.

I seem to see him, Nicola Laudìsi, in the dim room, tall, enormous, breathing heavily but without bending forward or getting flustered, stroking the servant woman's hair as one strokes the head of a dog.

That was how his wife saw him, and because she had nothing in her life—not even neighbors with whom to chat from her balcony toward evening—she decided to die. She confided in no one; she left no note (she barely knew how to write).

On Sunday morning she got dressed for mass and went out on the balcony. Since the curved railing might hamper her, or because she feared that since she was not very high above the street she might only be crippled and not killed, she saw she had no choice but to plunge headfirst. But, before that, she had to save her honor.

There were still no such things as safety pins. She took a dark, longish pin, the kind with a rounded head the color of black grapes. She pierced her skirt on two sides and bent the pin to close it. But she pricked her finger painfully and cried out.

Zulicchia appeared in the doorway. "Madam, what's the matter?"

"I cut myself," she said. "It's nothing." And she was left alone.

Taking tiny steps, hobbled as she was by the tight skirt, she reached the railing. She leaned out. She must have pushed hard with her elbows; with difficulty she managed to hang suspended, then fell. The street was deserted.

The pin held fast. Her ankles were just covered by the flowered skirt. My mother bent down to adjust it.

꞊

My mother said, "She was supposed to go to mass and she's gone to the Lord."

Nicola Laudìsi tottered and appeared about to collapse; Zulicchia and my mother, who barely came up to his shoulders, supported him on both sides.

"Kneel down, Alberto," my mother told me.

I knelt beside Aunt Clementina's head. I never thought I'd find myself so close to her.

On the tip of her forefinger there was still a drop of dark blood. Lighter blood now trickled from her skull toward one eyebrow. I took out the clean handkerchief my mother had put in my pocket and wiped her forehead. Then people started arriving.

Ignacia

Since the ice on the river had melted, it was thought feasible to go down to Viipuri by raft. The wedding of Princess Olympia had been set for the first Sunday in June, and the woodcutters and peasants attached to her mother's forests and cultivated fields were to converge on the castle no later than Saturday at sundown to take part in a celebration the likes of which, except for those of the czars, the waters that flow into the Baltic had not seen for a quarter of a century.

At that time in my youth, I was a guest of the old princess, the mother, whom I had met in Berlin and who had invited me along. But in the final days of the preparations, which were as sumptuous as you read about in fairy tales, baskets, fabrics, and cuttings of material were strewn over all the floors, while the palace corridors rang with orders and songs, and having diplomatically asked to be alone, I left on horseback for a wooded estate that my chatelaine, rich as Croesus, owned to the north and which was destined to form part of Olympia's dowry. Here, with the excuse of some sort of folklore research, I stayed for more than three weeks, living in a spacious cabin against whose window coverings the branches of the fir trees rustled when the wind touched them, as though stretched by the overload of snow they had held for too many months. A little farther down the woods thinned out and ended mysteriously on the shore of Pale Lake, from which flowed the beautiful Mir River, broad and navigable from its beginnings and the color of mother-of-pearl and opal even in sunlight, as though in its ripples it had caught the full moon. But you could barely make out the other shore of the lake, amid the Cimmerian mists and enchanted bleakness, and the inhabited earth appeared to end with those few cabins.

The men were bearded and wore furs; the women had limpid eyes and the tops of their cheeks were red, as if the bracing air had kissed them too hard. Their language, abounding in diphthongs, slipping and sliding between liquid consonants and sibilants, I found mysterious; to me it sounded so much like the twittering of strange birds that when the cuckoo began to sing again I caught myself smiling, almost as though I were hearing a familiar language, one I could repeat and understand syllable by syllable. The girls, in their way, were beautiful, Ignacia perhaps most of all, with her tight-fitting bodice, black and white like swallow feathers, her long silver filigree earrings, and those two kisses, or bites, imprinted high on her cheeks in the shape of two cherries. Sometimes, meeting me among the trees, she would greet me and begin a frank conversation, perhaps thinking that by dint of sympathy I might grasp the meaning of her words; then after a while, laughing, she went on her way.

Up there amid those tranquil people, I witnessed for the first time the wonder of the northern spring, when the crash of the ice as it breaks up is like a cry of joy and in the morning the woodcutter's ax, killing the trees he chops down, seems instead to be calling the whole forest to awaken and be born. In the new skies and short nights, the full moon of May was like a sun dimmed by sleep, a white sun of dreams.

Then the time came to go down to Viipuri.

There were twelve young women and twelve men. I went along with them. There was also an old man, the leader of the community, who stood in the stern of the raft and worked the rudder. The others stayed behind.

The raft was flat, made of long trunks crudely joined, and without sides. The men had oars but seldom used them. If we got too close to the bank, two or three men had only to lean effortlessly on the blade of their oars for the craft to correct its course. But generally it took only one if a log, among the many cut in the northern forest and floating downstream on their own toward the valley, caught by an eddy, bobbed up before us. The closest oarsman struck it with his oar and pushed it out of the way, and once again the current was ours, like a broad and deserted road.

The trip would take sixteen hours. We left as soon as it was daylight. For the first two hours the cold air, suffused with humidity through which the glassy clarity of the sky appeared, and the river, white as a milky way with its whirlpools that had the sound of distant sighs, kept us silent, each for himself as though continuing to sleep, curled up in blankets or enclosed in the black waterproof overcoats on which the dew glistened. From time to time, a bluish mist broke away from the trees barely covered by new greenery on the two banks of the river and was immediately lost; the sun, large, red, weak, was reluctant to rise above the rim of the horizon. All of a sudden, at a bend in the river, a ray of sunlight struck full on the water, stirring up a tumult of golden fish, smiled on the pallor of our faces, was mirrored on the copper cauldron that stood in the middle of the raft, and shone brightly. Whereupon one of the young men struck the gleaming copper with an iron rod, as though it were a gong greeting the sun, and immediately all twelve of them, six on each side, started rowing without needing to and singing "Aho! Ahoi!"

Then everything turned beautiful, and we all found our voices. We greeted one another, shaking hands like old acquaintances meeting after a long time on that raft, around which the waters themselves rejoiced by turning iridescent in the spray. The steersman's white beard looked like a god's. Then I saw the pile of wreaths that the forest girls were bringing as a gift to the bride, wreaths of dark fir, trimmed with pink and yellow paper flowers; and I saw, as though recognizing her for the first time, Ignacia, seated higher than her companions, not far from the rudder. She was sitting on the carved chest of light-colored wood, which contained the more precious gift, indeed the only gift of value that, along with those modest garlands, the families of the forest were sending to the bride: a large blue veil, studded with gold sequins in patterns representing the zodiac. Many women had worked on it, but Ignacia more than the others; and the design had been created by the same young man who had carved the chest, the artist Ilmari, who was standing next to me and who everybody said was soon to become her fiancé.

She wasn't looking at anyone; her round eyes, of a soft and indefinable color, were blissful; her face, unreddened that morning, was smooth and opaque like dark ivory, and her hands lay limply in her lap: those strange hands of hers, pale and elongated, so different from those of her girl companions, whose fingers were as thick and stumpy as mallets. I kept staring at her and only desisted when I became aware of Ilmari's hostile look.

Now the waters of the Mir were foaming in a narrow passage; the banks rose up, rocky and wooded, and we were again in the shade. The men, gripping the oars, kept silent and on the lookout for obstacles; and joy did not return until we had emerged once more into the open, already warm and radiant with sunshine. A flight of ducks, like a necklace of huge emeralds, crossed the width of the river, and we greeted it with shouts. Then someone lit an alcohol flame under the cauldron, and soon we were eating a steaming barley mush flavored with kümmel; we ate cold roast venison and drank bitter beer, and there were flasks of aquavit for those who wanted it. Now the sun was at its zenith and the singing began.

I knew the gist of one of the songs: "Dear spider, dear spider, come come, take take the maiden into the river, in the net of her hair, take take!" All eyes were turned on Ignacia, who had got to her feet and with the movement of her lips accompanied the song poured out by the others. All of a sudden, almost with one voice, they all started shouting "Ignacia!" and "Olympia!" and other enthusiastic words that I couldn't understand. Many hands pushed Ilmari toward the girl; other hands opened the chest and took out the blue and gold veil, a nocturnal sky shining against the sun. She looked serious, hardly smiling, but her hair fell to her shoulders, and she was wrapped in the veil beside her sweetheart. I would not have believed that such a wild and childish clamor could issue from their throats. They were celebrating in jest the wedding of Ignacia and Ilmari as though they were Olympia and her princely bridegroom; they tried to dance before them on the shaky raft; they sang, they shouted, they clapped their hands in rhythm. The couple stood silently in the rear, Ignacia motionless as an idol, almost on the far edge of the raft, to the right of the steersman.

I was the only one who heard a guttural cry from the steersman. The sun was hidden as we entered the churning narrows of Vaali. Perhaps none of them saw exactly what happened next, for they were all trying to keep their balance on the unsteady raft. I saw Ignacia lean out and extend her arm, either to support herself against the overhanging rock or to pluck a twig from a bush. A woodcock emerged from that bush, its blue wings fringed with white flapped against her hair, and it flew away. Ignacia had disappeared. Ilmari was left clutching the veil.

I heard a scream, a silence. The men, bent over the oars, shifted the raft away from the rock and turned it around; the women kept crying out sharply. Ignacia's hair emerged on the surface of the water; a corner of the raft must have struck her forehead. She was pulled under by the current, and the rushing water closed over her.

Then, after another cry, there was again silence. The current by now was calmer, and we floated downstream toward Viipuri, with one less, as the sun set behind our backs.

They kept silent for a long while, perhaps an hour or two. All of a sudden, like seagulls squawking toward evening, they all began yelling at once. I realized they were arguing angrily over who was to blame. Only Ilmari said nothing and beat his fists against his chest. Finally the steersman ordered them to shut up, and the silence was not broken again until we had almost arrived. But when the enlarged sun set on the gloomy horizon, they were afraid of solitude, and the oarsmen intoned "Aho! Ahoi!" but now it was a dirge. Then the women wept, and the eldest of them finally dared to approach the point on the raft where Ignacia's veil still lay, swelled by the breeze. She gathered it up, folded it slowly, kissed it, and put it back in the chest.

It was evening and the stars were out when we

arrived before the castle in Viipuri. The river there formed a broad basin, like a lake. A bare uphill stretch separated the shore from the castle. It rose in isolation, with its large transparent windows brightly lit. Seeing it from afar, anyone would have known that a wedding feast was in preparation.

We had lit a lantern on a pole at the prow of the raft.

The old princess was waiting for us on the landing. Two lackeys with torches stood by. She was waving a handkerchief.

When we had disembarked, the steersman and the eldest woman, almost kneeling before her ladyship, told her about the accident. She crossed herself and after a pause replied with a few excited words in their language. The woodcutters and women passed along the order.

"*Vous n'avez pas fait bon voyage, mon ami,*" she said to me, extending her hand to be kissed. "*C'est très regrettable.*"

And she added hastily, "*Il ne faut rien dire, absolument rien dire à Olympia. Elle ne pourrait pas supporter le mauvais augure. La pauvre!*"

We walked up toward the castle. The women followed, carrying the chest like a relic. The men brought up the rear.

The Window

Between my window and hers lay the road, the provin-
cial road where every so often the knife grinder halted
to pedal his clumsy device and Sundays at two the
tramp played his barrel organ, God knows for whom.
Usually the chirping sparrows hopped about on the
ground undisturbed, for it was a short thoroughfare,
and just hearing the sound of a bicycle was enough to
arouse my curiosity and make me look out the window; there were evenings when not even the barking of
a dog was to be heard, but only the grave humming of
the telegraph poles in the warm air, like the vibration
of an orchestra of tuning forks.

This was my last retreat. It was not the first; there
had been other times when I felt the wish to step back
from the current of life and stare at it, almost to relish

a vision of immortality. Other times I felt I was emerging on a riverbank from an exhausting swim to sit down on a stretch of dry gravel before which the flow of water and the flow of time proceeded like vain and musical things. But this was the last retreat; then life caught me once more in its toils and has never let me go. I had picked a little house, not much bigger than a matchbox, in an unfashionable rural area; and there since the beginning of April, which had been freezing cold, I had no other company but an old and untalkative manservant; no friends or women, month after month; almost no mail. I had a goodly supply of paper, which remained blank, and new books, uncut; I had above all a great wealth of fantasy, so luxuriant that I was unable to get a clear grasp of it, so richly flavored that I was carried away in silence, soaring within myself from adventure to adventure, dream to dream, with no goal and no ties and with the feeling that my existence was a smooth, elastic, reverberating surface. Ineffable well-being, like that of a boy or an ascetic! There were times when, watching the sun setting on the horizon of the plain, I seemed to see, to discover with my own eyes, that the world was round.

Across the road from my little house, the countryside was flat, almost treeless. The crops, especially when they shone in the sun after the rain, looked phosphorescent. Behind my house the slope of the first alpine spur was harsh and abrupt, so I almost never looked out on that side, and anyway I kept most of the rooms closed and spent my time only in the bedroom and in the study, which opened on a terrace facing the plain. From there and from the bedroom window I saw nothing but solitude, except for a run-down cottage still smaller than mine on the other side of the road. But even this house was strange and deserted or, later, when it was inhabited, strangely inhabited. The windows of its rooms all gave on the fields, and I couldn't see them; the facade on the road had six, in two rows, but they were fake and so badly painted, with greenish slats and yellowish smears, that not even the sparrows, at a distance of a hundred yards, would have taken them for real. A single window would have been visible on the narrower side of the little structure, which was as squeezed and cramped as a sentry box, but it was hidden from me by a dense, compact acacia tree with bushy foliage, impenetrable as a sphere, a cool, dark shadow that kept out even the hottest days.

So between the terrace where I walked, the window where I looked out, and that window, there was just the road and the acacia.

Her window. For a long time that's what I privately called it.

At first, for all of April and almost all of May, the cottage, which I called the sentry box, remained untenanted; indeed, this was one of the reasons, the certainty of having no neighbors, that had led me to choose this place. The owner of the cottage, a half-demented old maid tenderly enamored of a little gray bitch almost as old as she was, and obsessed by an extravagant fear of earthquakes, had been driven completely over the edge in the past couple of years by a kind of religious mania. The two servant women who kept her company had begun stealing from her on a grand scale; and finally some distant relatives had had her put away for good. For two years the real windows, closed at night, had looked more fake than the fake ones, while in the garden the brambles flourished.

But on one of the last mornings in May I heard not only the swallows flocking under those eaves—I also heard a flight of notes rising from an out-of-tune piano and wafting playfully over the countryside. And there was no mistaking where they came from. Later I learned that the sentry box had been rented to an old man and his daughter: he a shrunken little man, a smart dresser, dignified, wearing shabby, well-pressed suits that made him look even more diminished; she no longer a young girl, perhaps twenty-four, but young enough compared to him to seem more like his granddaughter than his daughter.

I did not inquire who they were or why they had come there. I hoped from the start that they'd soon go away, and I seldom encountered them on the road. We usually walked in opposite directions, and I was determined not to say hello if I happened to run into them. I stared at them with an almost insolent curiosity, which the daughter reciprocated, as if she wanted to burst out laughing in my face.

She was buxom and healthy, and one would have said that her beauty had been kneaded by the Creator in a hasty moment of high spirits. No line of her face could be considered finished and perfect; her dark hair, excessively abundant and gathered clumsily at the top, gave her a common look, which she accentuated with a scarf thrown over her shoulders; and even her body, tall and full, though upright on trim ankles, promised too much. Her ample cheeks and energetic chin were immoderate, except when filled out with a smile, and her dull dark complexion needed passion or hilarity in order to shine. I seldom saw her smile, but if she wasn't smiling, she often wore a peculiarly teasing expression of childish arrogance whose charm was equal to a smile. And her teeth, her eyes, were magnificent; her gaze, so forceful and electric, seemed to carry along with it the very eyes from which it originated!

Mornings and evenings I heard her bang the shutters of her window, invisible behind the acacia. She flung them open against the house or pulled them shut with a gesture I could imagine: as though she had awakened suddenly, without lethargy or languor, and was already thirsting for air or had gone to bed sweetly drowsy, no longer able to keep her eyes open. How much time did she spend at the window? Surely a lot—I had no way of knowing. At times I heard the usual flutter of notes from the piano, especially in merry competition with the barrel organ when it stopped between the two houses; but you could tell she was no pianist, and her playing was only an outlet; the chords spread outward in the solitude like the sound of her petulant laugh, which I hadn't heard. I can hardly say I had heard her voice. Once in a while, in all that time, I heard her call, stamping her heel in the doorway, "Papa! Papa!" when the old man was no doubt dawdling too long at getting himself dressed, but it wasn't her true voice; she was imitating—nasal and drawn out—the tone of *enfants gâtés* and mechanical dolls.

Side by side they would take their walk. Her beauty lay more in movement than in line. Her bust protruded, as though she found it hard to restrain herself and not run; every undulating, springing step was charged with unconsumed exuberance. When she passed under my window, she raised her eyes to look at me, openly, without flirtatiousness; if I was on the terrace, she looked me over from head to foot, the way you look at a tree that you recognize at a turn in the road.

I would find myself thinking of her. I imagined walking with her on my arm, shoulder to shoulder, while her old father and my old manservant followed at a distance. I enjoyed the symmetry. And then for days and days I'd forget about it.

Her father, still active at his age, departed for the city from time to time, leaving her alone for as much as half the week. Then all went on as before, except that she did not look up when passing beneath my window. In the afternoon she took a walk toward the hill or sat with a book on the path through the chestnut trees behind my house. I would get a glimpse of her. Often she would rest her cheek on her hand, or pass her hand through her hair, like a woman who knows her own body and loves it and waits leisurely for others to love it as well.

Then when the old man came back, her voice when she called him—"Papa!"—the first day was perhaps slightly different from the one I knew, perhaps less joking. And they resumed their walks along the level road.

Since from the beginning I had not said hello to them, now I couldn't decide to. And our eyes would meet and stop: hers without intent, mine without concern.

I'm not one of those people who dread autumn. The colors of the countryside make it the most festive of seasons, and there is the smell of the winepress. I stayed on until early November, as did they. But after All Souls' Day the father went to the city and was to return only to pack up and leave.

The acacia shed its leaves, first little by little, then more quickly. First I saw only the upper slats of the shutters; then I began to see her black hair when she was looking out the window. But one night it was windy, and it was still windy in the early morning, and the golden yellow leaves fluttered and fell. No longer was the acacia between my window and hers; there was only the road.

She came to the window and I saw her face. But this time I didn't see her hair. The few leaves left on the acacia crowned her forehead from afar, like a crown of pale gold. Our eyes met, and mine, I think, were unrestrained. She withdrew, and a flurry of notes rose from the piano like a flight of crazy leaves.

So I went down, just as I was, and knocked at her door.

"Who is it?" came her true voice.

"It's me."

She led me into a small drawing room, and I sat down beside her. Her bosom rose as she breathed, and she pushed her hair back from her forehead. Up close her complexion looked even darker. Then she started laughing, her laugh of a conceited child.

I took her hand without knowing what I was doing; she became serious and withdrew her hand.

"Be nice! What did you come here for?"

"I came to ask you . . . your name."

She laughed again. "Erminia."

"Erminia among the shady trees," I said stupidly.

"The trees aren't shady anymore," she said. "Are you staying here all winter? We go back to the city on Saint Martin's Day."

"I'm leaving the day after," I said immediately. "Or the same day." And again I took her hand.

Then she stopped laughing.

Thus life caught me in its toils and has never let me go.

Love

Her girlish love for Viganò was the most beautiful thing in her life—this, she said, was what she'd been born for—but even he, who had known the world, was unable to recall anything finer.

Not too late on a September afternoon, along the deserted beach beyond Fiumetto, he all of a sudden felt young in a way he would never have believed possible. To his left was the Tyrrhenian Sea, already sunless at this spot, clear and fresh as glazed porcelain; to his right the pine grove, now dark, and the radiant outline of the Apuan Alps, resembling the Dolomites come to look at the sea. But also on his right and much closer was Marta Aymi, dark and as tall as he was; and with her long tennis player's strides she kept pace with him. Sometimes as they walked, they were up to their bare ankles in the low tide; they kept going for a while and emerged running to seek out with their feet a place where the sand was still warm. Looking straight ahead, hurrying to reach Forte dei Marmi in time to get dressed for dinner, they spoke bantering words that almost flew before them like their long shadows or the little clouds of golden sand that they kicked up with every step.

But then the words turned serious, as though wanting to stop and put down roots. They themselves stopped and looked at each other. Each had the impression of seeing the other's eyes for the first time, and this astonished them. Actually it was the man who was astonished, since a woman almost always knows what she wants. Her shining hazel eyes were new to him, as though at that very moment the tender skin of the eyelids had opened, with those tiny bottomless abysses of the black pupils and that restrained quiver of the eyelashes, which made him lose his way. He felt perplexed, quick to think how ridiculous he looked with his bare feet and the sandals dangling from his belt. It was she who put her trembling hand on his shoulder, and they kissed for a long time without saying a word.

So far she knew very little about him. His fame as an architect, achieved mostly in America and Russia and only indirectly known in Italy, was not of the kind to resonate much in a middle-class family; his economic status was not apparent; his face was quite youthful, but his hair, scant and no longer wholly blond, betrayed his years. All the girl knew specifically was that he had a wife and children, and she had met them, since they were staying with him in the same hotel where she and her parents were, and she saw that his family life was good and perfect. Yet, one evening in August, as he entered the lounge crowded with vacationers, she caught his eye and in her thoughts isolated him from everyone else. Later she kept on the lookout for him; she drew closer to him in September when the guests began to thin out; she lured him out on long walks; finally, that day, she kissed him. So it was love, without calculation and without hope, the kind that men seek like the philosophers' stone. A woman is almost always able to believe that she is loved for herself, but a man never knows whether women choose him for himself, his money, his name, or his reputation in society. This was a disinterested love and therefore simple and pure. Viganò felt illuminated by it and shaken, his conscience so clear that had he obeyed his instinct, he would have quickened his pace in order to tell his wife about his happiness.

Instead he was prudent, like someone who has found a jewel and would like to contemplate it at least for a few days before giving it up. It had to be given up. The Aymis—a whole tribe of parents, children, aunts and uncles, cousins—were irreproachable people. Marta herself was irreproachable, indeed inaccessible, having reached the age of twenty-five without finding any of the many men who had courted her to her liking. It was her misfortune and joy, which thrilled her, to have fallen in love with someone who could not be her husband and *must* not be her lover. As for Viganò, he had old-fashioned ideas: love was born and bloomed with a delight in beautiful things that must soon vanish, like clouds dispersing or a mirage that enchants without deceiving.

It lasted a little over a week, the close of a season. They took some short boat rides, walked among the pines, stopped to rest on the grass; he was so childish as to lay his head on her knees as she sat, and with her long fingers she closed his eyes. She also gave him kisses, ever more difficult to understand, like rare fruits from the top of an autumnal tree. Her lips became reluctant, not from remorse but for fear of giving consistency to something fleeting and already over, and because she was beginning to feel more disturbed in her blood than she would have liked.

Her mother and an uncle were suspicious and discussed it between them. But they were content merely to keep an eye on her, trusting in the girl and the man's seriousness and their imminent separation. They wrote to each other from afar, but the letters were too restrained to arouse any passions. But since the correspondence gave signs of being prolonged, the mother managed to intercept Viganò's letters before they reached her daughter; and Marta, after scolding him two or three times for his silence, stopped writing. But she became sad and capricious.

Two years went by, and a marriage proposal came along, the best imaginable. She would hear nothing of it, saying, "I don't want him, and I don't want anyone else. It's too late. I don't want a husband. I've made up my mind."

Nothing could dissuade her. Then a family council

was held, and Bruno, the uncle who had guessed the situation at Forte dei Marmi, had an idea.

He left for Viganò's city and had himself announced. He walked the length of the studio, looking at nothing; he went up to Viganò and looked him straight in the eye. He knew that by now the architect's fame had grown at home as well, that he was influential and scrupulous; he could talk to him.

Viganò's questions were conventional and at the same time embarrassed. "You, here? Commendator Martini? Uncle . . . if I remember correctly . . . brother. Is everyone all right? It's been so long since I've had any news."

"Marta's uncle," he replied. "Her mother's brother. Everyone's fine. Marta is engaged . . . she's supposed to be engaged," he corrected himself, observing the emotion that the other had been unable to repress in time.

He explained the circumstances fully: the advantages offered by the match; Marta's age and situation; the need that she accept; the stubborn and mysterious nature of her refusal; in general, her sadness and the way she had been pining away for the past two years; the distress of her parents, now old and anxious to see their daughter's life properly arranged. Finally he expressed the firm opinion that the intervention of a serious man, one who had "influence" over the girl, could be providential, and he invited him to spend a few days with them, immediately, at Valtellina.

The novelty of the situation, the strange and

sudden request, the wish to see a landscape he didn't know and the woman who had been dear to him, the fear of being blamed for a destiny gone awry and held responsible for a life, the need to avoid more delicate explanations with this extraordinary visitor—all these reasons, and no other reason but a fantastic impulse, induced him to say yes. Only when he was there did he realize the absurd position into which they had forced him.

Meanwhile, it was indispensable that his intervention, if it was to have the desired result, should be skillful and gradual. And so the mother, the uncle, and a few other family members who had more or less been let in on the secret encouraged his meetings with Marta; they practically arranged them for him and then withdrew at the right moment. The flirtation was fully resumed with an ardent and melancholy impetus that terrified him. After a few days the girl told him all about the marriage proposal and stated her vow: Since she couldn't belong to the man she loved, she wouldn't belong to anyone. Then he began to persuade her. Surprised, suspecting that he might be thinking of sharing her in an arrangement with her future husband and recalling a frivolous remark he had once made on the beach, she paused, trembling, and exclaimed, "I'm not that kind of woman."

Viganò appeared offended, and he really was offended. He took her back, still arguing and protesting, to the hotel.

The next morning Marta arrived for the rendezvous with reddened eyes. She had been crying, having talked herself into the sacrifice so as not to make her old parents suffer. She hugged him passionately, "for the last time," beseeching him never to try to see her again.

What had ruined her life was the vanity, the meanness, the stupidity, of everyone. Such was her judgment now that her life, once so clear and beautiful, had become a filthy thing. Had she openly blamed herself as well, she would not have been able to stand it. Her resentment drew no distinctions among her husband, Viganò, her mother, and the rest of the family. As for Uncle Bruno, the one who had had "the idea," she wanted nothing more to do with him; she would not allow him in her house, and when she met him on the street she stared at him without saying hello. He said he thought his niece had gone crazy.

From the start, the fiancé, pleased that the bride's family was on intimate terms with someone famous, wanted him as best man at the wedding, and Viganò was unable to refuse. Since he was a fashionable architect, the fiancé-turned-husband commissioned him to design the new villa, with two verandas and a tower; and since in his youth he had also been a painter, he pressured him into painting Marta's portrait: a mediocre performance, but the sittings lasted all summer. Having learned, through a heedless remark by his mother-in-law, that Viganò had helped Marta to make up her mind, the husband considered him a paternal friend, though he was less than ten years his senior; he kept him abreast of the squabbles with his wife, confided in him the smallest details of their conjugal life, and bestowed on him the office of adviser and peacemaker. One day, after one of these quarrels, which had become almost daily, she burst furiously into a drawing room where Viganò was lying on a sofa reading, and crying in a choked voice "The two of you, the two of you . . . you!" she hurled herself on him as though to strangle him. He took her, brutally, in that room where even a servant might have come in at any moment.

He would have liked to run away at once, but it seemed despicable to abandon her, and though she thought she hated him more than she loved him, she clung to him so that they might sink together. Their relationship was unrestrained, almost public. It was as though they were hoping for a tragic solution, with Marta trying, no matter how, to bring this shame to an immediate and liberating end. Instead it went on and on. The mother—for fear of scandal or tragedy and out of remorse at having accepted Bruno's idea—did her best to cover up the affair, and the moral standing of the Aymi family, once spotless, suffered accordingly. The two younger girls, still unmarried, felt enveloped by a soiled reputation and hated their sister.

She, with the wish for death forever springing up in her heart, succeeded only in aging more rapidly. She fell dangerously ill with typhus but recovered. Her lover entered the room where she lay, her fever having abated. "Now life begins again," he said, stroking her cropped hair.

"Yes," she replied, averting her eyes, "now it begins again, this filthy business—life!"

It was her bitter whim to want to finish her convalescence at Forte dei Marmi.

They were both sitting on a balcony before evening: he by now loaded with titles and honors but hopelessly old and tired, convinced that his art was worth no more than a dry leaf. He who had built towers and verandas for others felt only an idle wish to dig a hole and bury himself. Little by little, his family had dispersed; his children were grown and on their own; his wife for most of the year went to live with the nuns. Only Marta's husband remained in the dark.

Marta sat cooling herself with a feather fan, though there was no need to. It disgusted her that she had put on weight during her recovery, and she had the idea that cosmetics spoiled her looks.

The time and the season were the same as before. The sea was the same with its fresh evening glaze, and the mountains of rose-colored marble. One would have said that even the grains of sand on the beach were the same. All that was missing on the sand were the swift, light shadows, the bare, almost dancing feet, of two people who in a September sunset had invented love.

Bianca

Twenty years ago—I'm now thirty-nine—I was in Florence, where my family had sent me to study. I had quit technical school for the Liceo, and the final exams did not go well. In July, twenty years ago, I failed two subjects; but I worked hard during vacation and in October got my diploma *de haute lutte,* as I said to myself. It seemed to me I deserved a grand prize, and so I became Bianca's lover. I sported a little blond beard *à la française,* a bowler hat, gloves held smartly folded in the palm of the hand, and a bamboo walking stick. Sometimes, looking in the mirror, I pondered whether or not to adopt a monocle.

It was an adventure, without qualms, my excuse being that Bianca was three years older than I and a teacher, or, as they said in those days, an emancipated woman. But the fact remains that she was a respectable young lady, and I had met her at the home of distant relatives to whom I'd been introduced by my father. Indeed, the first time we touched hands without clasping them was the very evening of my Liceo diploma, when my hosts, by the light of the oil lamp, uncorked a bottle of sweet wine in my honor. She asked nothing of me, and I promised her nothing. There seemed to be all the time in the world for us to examine our feelings in depth and to act accordingly. My father, however, quickly found out about the situation, summoned me home, and made me transfer to the most distant university he could find. We exchanged letters, not many. It was easy to convince myself that I was a kid, with no responsibility or blame, and that it was up to her to exercise prudence. Once in a while remorse awakened me at night, like a thief entering the bedroom, but then it left me in peace. And I felt wholly relieved when, during the next year's vacation, my father indirectly informed me that Bianca had stopped teaching and married a successful professional man.

So I hardly thought about it anymore. I remember only that I couldn't read or hear the old expression "first love" without a feeling of discomfort, almost a hectic flush, a malaise that gets under your skin like shame. It struck me as an aversion to clichés, and I immediately dismissed it.

The period of our love was November and December. I was living in a second-floor furnished room on the rather dark and noisy Via Porta Rossa; she over toward San Gallo, where she taught school. Florence at the time had horse-drawn omnibuses, very high and large and gloomy, or at least that's how I remember them. Certainly they were painted a less than cheerful color, a blue verging on black that in the foggy autumn could actually look black. They provided service from the city gates to the center, and the team of two horses trotted at the same slow pace that brought pretentious folk in their carriages from the suburbs to the central market. The driver was so high up that from a distance he seemed to be seated, his legs dangling, on the roof of the vehicle, and from up there he hadn't the slightest wish to yell at the carriage drivers, through whose midst he passed as though piloting a battleship in a swarm of light surface craft. On his shoulders he wore a round cloak, blue black, and his hat must have been about the same color, flat like a boater, but covered with oilskin, and with the brim rolled up in an odd fashion at the sides.

Inside the omnibus were two long, narrow benches, likewise covered in shiny black oilcloth. What little light there was entered from the window of the door, and it was bleak even on fine days. I never boarded the omnibus. In the square there usually alighted little old men and women, petit bourgeois types convinced it was worth spending two soldi for the omnibus to save wear and tear on their shoes.

Bianca, looking so young, came last, having let the others disembark first. She would smile at me in exhaustion, as though arriving from a long journey; and she accepted the hand I offered her to help her descend the two steps of the high and shaky footboard. Often under her woolen cape with its cheap fur collar and trimmings I glimpsed a strange dress she wore, all black, rather loose at the waist, going down to her ankles, and adorned, if that is the right word, with a few rows of sequins. Her face, in its humility, was exquisitely beautiful, but to me it looked too sad.

In the thin drizzle, or the twilight, her smile was paler still. I was struck by the thought that I might lose her in the crowd and never find her again.

Upstairs, in the room, she was a little out of breath from climbing the steep stairs. There she would some-times grasp my temples between her cold, tense hands, seeking to understand me by gazing into the whites of my eyes.

"My boy!" she would say. "My naughty boy! Soon you'll go off on your own."

Thus she spoke and kissed me with her thin lips.

I think that more than anything else there was soli-tude in her heart.

The years went by. I had gone off on my own. I had settled in this city, with a wife and children, and had, as they say, done well.

For many years I lost track of time. For me it was as though nothing existed but tomorrow; I didn't even linger over the present, allowing it to pass like sand through the fingers in pleasant anticipation of the next day. I had yet to discover the past.

That was what happened to me one evening just this last winter—all of a sudden, as one says of a vase filled drop by drop until it begins to overflow on all sides. Thinking about it later, I had the feeling that memory is something cold and vast, a shadow, or a dark stretch of water, that spreads and takes up the whole space where before there had been sun.

It was one evening, a little before falling asleep. My heart, as I began to doze off, gave me the feeling of a trot, slower and slower, either transporting me or approaching me. And then, from the trotting, there emerged the image of a vehicle, large, high, gloomy, with wheels without tires and with the hooves of its two horses beating on the pavement. I am standing in the square. It is drizzling. Now the hearse too has stopped. Yes, the hearse! In my nocturnal vision, even what little color it had has vanished, that suggestion of dark blue; and the Florentine omnibus, with the cloaked driver sitting on top, is for all intents and purposes a hearse, except that at the open door, its footboard still wobbly from the last jolt on arriving, there appears and alights I don't say a shy young woman but a smile, Bianca's smile, mild and bright as untarnished gold, a ray of pure sunlight at dusk, something dead and immortal.

I understand what has happened in me. I've reached the summit of my life, and now I'm starting on the downward path. The rivers of time are now rushing before me along the other slope; they descend toward the shadows.

Hiding under the blankets, I'd prefer not to look. But that inextinguishable and immortal smile is before me. Bianca neither disappears nor steps down from the footboard of the omnibus, and her smile is inviting. I shudder; I sit up in bed, almost suffocated. I should like to call out to someone for help, but not to the woman lying there next to me. I should like to hear, spoken with the voice of the past, the whispered words that tremble here and there in the darkness: "Boy, boy! You'll go off on your own."

Now I feel immersed in the river of time, carried away, submerged. Oh, if only I could cling to the shore! Get free of the current! Preserve only a moment of fleeting life, even if it's this bitter moment right now! To clutch the edge of a stone, a clump of grass, a single blade of grass through which gleams, on the motionless riverbank, the smile of this dying sun!

In a cold sweat my anxiety subsides. Sleep finally enfolds me like a shroud.

The days were untroubled. Two nights in a row the vision returned.

On the third day I had a committee meeting. No sooner were we seated than the chairman announced, "We won't wait for Commendator X. His wife is seriously ill."

Our interest was piqued. Without moving from the table, the chairman picked up the telephone and asked, "Can you give me any news of Signora Bianca?" After a pause he turned to us and said, "It looks hopeful again."

"I didn't know he was married," I said. "Who is his wife?"

The others explained to me vaguely. They weren't sure about the past. They knew he had got married many years before in Florence. The eldest daughter was sixteen or seventeen years old.

I didn't know this man very well but enough to call him later from my office and ask him for news myself. I asked the chairman for special assignments, I sought ways to enter into direct relations with him, to visit him in his office, and to telephone him at home. Sometimes my persistence aroused his suspicions, but he could find no grounds for them.

For two months Bianca's condition stopped improving and she suffered a relapse; she leaned out toward death but turned aside. But no day went by without my somehow having news of her, and whenever I was most anxious, I often managed to hear something twice a day. They lived on a quiet and solitary street in the direction of the public gardens. I walked back and forth in that neighborhood at hours when I could be sure of not meeting the husband; and it seemed to me that a large hearse, high and dark like the Florentine omnibus, might soon draw up in front of the door.

Instead the snow was shoveled from the pavement; the primroses bloomed in the city; and when the sky was overcast, the new leaves on the trees shone as though illuminated from within. In March Bianca began to recover.

"When she's well," I said to her husband, "you'll surely have a celebration."

"Could be!" he said. "Bianca will have one even if she's not completely well. As soon as she can travel I'm taking her to Tuscany. This climate is not for her."

From others, I later learned they were giving an Easter supper for close friends and would leave in three days for Marina di Pisa.

On Easter Monday I posted myself at the gate of the public gardens and surveyed her street with my eyes.

The sky was so mild that it seemed impossible there were still no swallows.

She emerged around eleven, holding the hand of her youngest child, who could not yet have been ten years old; leaning on him for support but without seeming to, she walked in my direction. I was not afraid of hurting her and stationed myself at a spot where she couldn't help seeing me. I look much the same as in previous times, except that my eyes are no longer so bold.

She recognized me and blushed. She let go of her son's hand and held tightly to his arm.

Since she didn't immediately lower her eyes, I greeted her by lifting my hat. I saw that her hair was gray, but her eyebrows, and the softness of her cheeks, were the same as before. I trembled and waited. She, going pale, made up her mind and returned my greeting, smiling to herself. Then she tugged her little boy and proceeded quickly on her way.

Her smile had already waned; the frail blade of grass, transparent with sunlight, that I had clutched at for a moment had slipped from my fingers. A group of people pouring out of the gardens came between us and surrounded me like a vortex.

Looks

". . . exquisite styling, soberly elegant furnishings; a clear play of light and color that lifts the spirit and invites you to relax in quiet and comfort . . . this is what the Music and Conversation Lounge offers the passenger on the most beautiful of Italian steamships, the *Alcione*. Everything contributes to the pleasure of the eye in the most luxurious surroundings; the comfortable armchairs with soft cushions; plants and flowers. . . ."

Husband and wife had paused in the music and conversation lounge with the friend who had taken them on a tour of the ship and was leaving at dusk for Argentina. There was no music and too much conversation: that dim and discordant chatter, that coarse succession of prolonged murmurings broken suddenly by a strident exclamation, that false gaiety and ostentatious sorrow, that thronging and dispersal of groups of travelers and well-wishers, in short all that unseemly hubbub that makes an ocean liner about to sail resemble a market square or the lobby of a courthouse or any of those places and occasions where humanity is at its least attractive in being seen and heard.

"I'm going up and get some air," said Marzi, stopping in the middle of the lounge. "Anyone care to join me?"

But his wife, smiling, replied, "I'm a bit tired. I'll wait for you here. Vittorio, will you keep me company?"

He went back up on deck while the others sauntered toward the rear of the lounge. He stood for a while, leaning on the railing and gazing at the lights that came on one by one in the dusk, the green one at the lighthouse, the pale red ones on the harbor vessels, the yellower ones of the city, lights of all colors that made the hills disappear and hid the stars. Then he was suddenly struck by the notion that those lights were confused and provoking, like the voices in the lounge, and he felt bothered by the sirocco, which blew steadily, punctuated at almost equal intervals by the evening chill.

Then, slowly, his hands behind his back, he returned to the lounge; but the entrance was blocked by a group of people, which made him hesitate and held him back. The interior, however, was almost deserted, flooded by electric light; and as he waited for a path to open through the little crowd, so as not to have to ask permission or elbow his way through, he could look for a few moments—and they were very long moments—at his wife and their friend sitting in a corner at the rear.

She was seated on one of those comfortable armchairs with soft cushions; the man, not particularly close, on the end of a leather sofa; and they were neither looking at each other nor exchanging words. But he, Vittorio, was looking at the woman with a steady, silent gaze, more luminous than all the lamps, that rested on her cheek like the sunlight of a long afternoon on a rose-colored slope. She herself was looking straight ahead, her eyes empty and distracted; but she could hardly have been unaware of the force and light of that gaze from which her face took color.

Marzi stood for a moment in disbelief, questioning whether what he was seeing was simply an effect of all those glittering lamps. Then he moved noiselessly toward them; he stopped just over halfway and was about to call out "Amalia!" But at that moment she saw him and said, "Here's Gino." She spoke in a natural voice and made only a slight movement of her chin toward their friend, who shifted his gaze from her to her husband. But she appeared to have merely put aside that gaze, the way you put aside (in order to take it up again later) some familiar and obedient object, the way your hand lays aside the letter you're writing or the book you're reading when someone comes to call.

"So you're back," Vittorio said simply.

Soon it came time for farewells. As husband and wife prepared to disembark, she felt cold and muffled herself up; then she was afraid of stumbling on the gangplank and clung to his arm. Because she had been so weak as to shiver with a little fresh air, because she had been afraid and had relied on him for support, he once again felt secure. And he was delighted to hear her say in a perfunctory voice "Thanks, dear."

Their friend spent two years in Argentina; he came back for a brief visit and departed again for other far-away places, reappearing unexpectedly from time to time.

The memory of that twilight on the *Alcione* also reappeared sometimes in Marzi's mind, like the memory of a momentary frenzy. But if he had been jealous for a moment, it meant that his blood was infected by the sickness; and he kept forcing himself to forget while fearing, from one day to the next, that something might happen to spark a relapse. Besides, it seemed to him that among all the varieties of moral decay, the evil of jealousy was one of the saddest and most shameful, with a general tendency to become chronic unless a rare miracle brought a cure or an almost equally rare stroke of luck made it certain that one had been self-deceived. It was something tortuous and mean in any case and in his own case absolutely inadmissible. For he and Vittorio had been companions since elementary school and had spent almost all the Sundays of their adolescence together. He was not a friend, he was *the* friend. And then Amalia, the plump little girl with her hair hanging loose on her shoulders who lived in the next villa at Lido d'Albaro—didn't everyone at the time jokingly call her his sweetheart? Friendship and love had kept his boyhood alive for him; the doubt now tarnishing them was corrupting the most beautiful things in his life.

An alarmed imagination, that evening on the *Alcione,* had cast a fantasy on his mind, like a monstrous shadow on a wall. This same imagination, reined in by caution and guided by hope, might lead him to a paltry truth. Vittorio's gaze, her steadiness, were not to be doubted. But wasn't it likely (or certain) that he, swayed by melancholy feelings of departure, had been looking at this woman, who might even be innocently dear to him, without actually seeing her, the way one watches a shoreline recede on the horizon? And that she, a bit tired as she had said, was lost in the void, without a thought for anything? When the soul is caught in such nets, one would like for it all to be translated into words, words that may be brutal, lethal, but at least have a precise meaning. Looks in the eyes are instead like music, which stirs the heart but cannot be translated into exact words.

Between these shifting moods years went by. Amalia became lovelier than ever; slimming down had made her look taller; and her pale face had acquired pride, with her hair covering her forehead like a cloud. And finally came the summer when Marzi, having built a villa high in the mountains, moved into it from the nearby hotel where he and his wife had stayed for a few weeks overseeing the final construction. The official housewarming took place one evening in August with a supper to which they had invited half a dozen friends.

But the weather that August day had been the finest of the season, and a party of sightseers, among

them Amalia and Vittorio, had left in the early morning on an excursion to the Colle della Vedetta. Marzi
had deliberately stayed behind, citing his usual distaste
for walking and the wish to supervise certain finishing
touches on the new house. But actually he was in the
grip of an absurd need to suffer, and once he was alone,
he realized it. The frenzy against which he had been
struggling for so long erupted in his soul, and he found
no relief except in letting himself be devastated by it
without putting up any resistance. He regretted not
having gone along with the others and was glad that he
hadn't; he reevoked minute details of the past, enlarg-
ing them to huge certainties; he decided that Amalia
hadn't insisted enough on having his company; he
went and looked out the window twenty times as
though the mountain that the others were invisibly
climbing might reveal everything to him. Finally, he
settled on this thought: If when she comes back, she's
affectionate and talkative, if she clings to my arm as she
did that evening, then there's no more reason for suspicion.

Instead she returned silent and worn out and had
little to say at the table. But during supper the story of
the hike came out from other lips. When the time had
come to return, opinions were divided: some—Amalia
and Vittorio and another young lady, to be exact—had
wanted to descend by the steep and rocky canyon; the
others had preferred the path. But ten minutes after
they had started down, the girl complained that her
feet and knees hurt and climbed back up diagonally to
rejoin the others. The pair had pursued their breakneck
course; Amalia had become quite fatigued; having

reached the meadow, they rested and waited for the rest of the party.

They drank champagne to toast the new house. She clinked glasses with her husband and the guests without looking anyone in the face. Whereupon he murmured an excuse to get up from the table first and from a darkened room peered at what was going on in the dining room. Strange: the last ones to move to the drawing room were his wife and their friend; and she, passing ahead of Vittorio, gave him a look that could hardly be one of courtesy and greeting but that seemed to her husband interminable, full of contempt, pain, and reproach. What sort of look was it if not that of a woman at a man who has overcome her resistance, or at least made the attempt?

One of the ladies tried out the new piano by playing Chopin. He fled to his room, barely able to contain himself, feeling Chopin's most desperate prelude coursing in his veins. He tried to sleep, trusting that somehow the serenity of the morning would bring down his fever and let him perceive the truth. But he awoke in the half light of dawn, and there before his eyes was the same enigma, gray and indecipherable.

The third look came a few months later in a hospital room after he had undergone an operation. His wife was there beside him. The door opened and there stood Vittorio, whom they had not seen since the summer. He hesitated on the threshold, looked first at the woman without greeting her, then looked at him.

Wasn't it obvious that he had looked at her to find

out if there was truly no more hope of saving his friend? And how could there be any question of Amalia's grief? Everything was obvious, and nothing; nothing and everything were to be questioned.

By now, however, it was no longer worth combating these dark phantasms. The doctors had become aware of the sickness devouring his flesh only when it had become incurable; no one was aware of the cancer of jealousy that had destroyed his soul. He was taking the secret with him.

He had imagined being able to approach the end with a mild curiosity. Instead he still had the strength to turn away in bed and stare at the white wall. With eyes closed he again saw the tumult of lights on the *Alcione;* he heard once more the underground music of Chopin. He was thinking that so violent an emotion might break the lingering ties with life and bring on the long sleep wherein perhaps lay the truth and certainly peace.

The *Secrétaire*

"Whatever I have my children will divide in peace. My children are equal. Your mother doesn't play favorites. But the *secrétaire* must go to Egidio. What good is it to you?" she asked, turning to her three daughters. "Your brother will be able to use it."

"No good to us at all," replied her daughters, smiling. "Egidio can have the *secrétaire*. But why do you go on and on about it, Mamma? You'd think you were about to die any minute. As though that piece of furniture were worth all that much."

And so Egidio inherited the fine Empire piece— much sooner than anyone would have thought. For his mother died almost unexpectedly on a summer night after an hour of heart spasms. And no one had taken her seriously when, from time to time, she used to say that one day she'd simply collapse, "drop dead." And everyone, meeting her with her three girls, repeated the compliment that she seemed like their sister, if ever so slightly older, the usual compliment to which she listened with a smile tinged with modesty, a touch of satisfaction, and a touch of self-pity.

They were all together—mother, son and daughters, daughter-in-law, grandchildren—at a mountain resort. That day she had wanted to climb a peak, and only on returning, when the wind hit her at the top of a hill, did she go strangely pale and put her hand to her breast. Later, after some hot tea and a drop of cognac, she felt restored. But at midnight the hotel was thrown into confusion by the sound of ringing bells, cries and sobs, and the protests, immediately stilled, of the other vacationers.

Gasping on the bed, surrounded by her whole family, who hung back to let her breathe, she could say only four words. The first were "I'm dying." Then, motioning her son closer with a frantic gesture of her hands, she said to him point-blank, "The *secrétaire* . . ."

"The *secrétaire*," he replied, "I know you're leaving it to me eventually, Mamma, but you're going to be all right, Mamma. . . ."

Writhing, she shook her head and choked back words impossible to utter. She seemed to be asking for paper on which to write but was unable to hold the pencil in her already clenched fingers. Then the priest arrived to murmur the phrases and go through the gestures of his ministry without her being able to respond.

A little later she again had the strength to open her eyes, which glistened from a sleep from which there is no awakening, and to move her lips.

"I'm burning," she said, or so it seemed to Egidio and the others.

He brought a glass of water to his mother's lips. But her head fell back and she expired.

Many stars fell and expired that night, the night of Saint Lawrence.

They returned to the city at once; and the autumn was dark and soon over. Had his wife not persuaded him, Egidio would never have made up his mind to remove the *secrétaire* from the house where his mother had lived and where his three sisters and an aunt now remained. He had it transported to his study and stopped his ears to keep from hearing the dismal, empty thuds as the moving men pushed it to the wall; he turned away so as not to see it, for in the drizzly afternoon the polished mahogany looked almost black, and its gilded bronze fittings made it darker still.

He was thirty years old, and until that summer it had been his good fortune never to witness death. He had been far away, on a school trip, when his father had fallen sick; and by the time he reached home his mother and sisters were already wearing mourning. Later he read in a book that there are two great sorrows: that of the mother who loses her child and that of the son who loses his mother. He could imagine the grief of the mother losing her child and saw no difference between one parent's torment and the other's, since it took only a touch of whooping cough in his little boy to drive him out of his mind with worry—and indeed his wife had taken it much more calmly than he. But of the other sorrow, that of the son for his mother, he had had no inkling, and he accused himself of having a cold heart because he had been unable to imagine this future anguish. Remorsefully he recalled that for the death of his father he had felt only a long and immutable sadness, almost the incurable regret of not getting to know him well and love him like a friend, that reserved and secretive man with indecipherable thoughts in his eyes and a remote smile on his lips. But how could he fear, how could he even think of losing his mother—this woman who, except for the aftermath of giving birth, had never been ill a day in her life and certainly spoke of dropping dead because she had no idea what illness was? He had sometimes happened to recognize her from a distance on the street, she ahead of him, he walking far behind in the same direction. He recognized her by her brisk and steady pace, by the smooth cut of her street clothes gathered at a waist like that of a young girl. Then he would quicken his step to catch up with her and make her turn around by proudly calling out "Mamma!" When she blushed with surprise and pleasure, her face glowed like a coal under the ashes of her warm, gray hair.

And now she was gone, vanished, as though snatched away by the hand of an assassin. At first he felt nothing but a dry wrenching pain, a lament without tears, for he had no tears. Next his distress gradually deepened until it became physically unbearable, an inner void, a bitter insatiable hunger that at times made him want to howl. And always the despair of not having grieved enough. For long weeks he was apprehensive, in expectation of another misfortune, another disaster, as if fate had now discovered the path leading to his house. And at the same time it seemed to him that he no longer loved his wife and children, that he felt no joy in them—the gifts of life that remained to him had no value compared to what he had lost.

Time went by, cloaking the past with its consolations, as cold and transparent as a slow inundation of water. It finally came to pass that Egidio even decided to use the *secrétaire,* with its many drawers and secret nooks and crannies, the ingenuous whims of a cabinet-maker who had concealed an opening under a molding. It could now be talked about in his presence like any other piece of furniture.

"It's lovely, it's harmonious," his wife said one day. "But too bad that safe manufacturers have started imitating the Empire style. All they've done is to cheapen it for pieces like this. . . . Not all the bronze fittings are authentic."

"The ones on the columns are," said Egidio, admiring the meticulous little capitals.

At this point their little boy chimed in; he was only just learning to read but enjoyed being told adventure stories.

"If the columns were full of gold coins, Papa, how much would it be?"

He made a rough mental calculation and, smiling, stood up and tapped his fingernail against a wooden column.

"Empty," he told the child. "Grandma wasn't rich."

He stayed up late that night, alone in his study, with no wish to do anything and no desire to sleep. At a certain point he got up from his chair and unwittingly tapped once more on the two columns with his fingernail, as he had done in the afternoon in the presence of his wife and son. He began to examine the small bronze crowns that served as capitals and saw that they ended in little hooks of the same, almost indistinguishable, color. Then it occurred to him that the wood of each column had sounded different when tapped with his finger. He tried to force one of the hooks; the bronze foil unwound like a ribbon, and the column turned. He pulled it out, and it was empty; he heard only the rattle of some worm-eaten splinters that broke off inside. Slowly he put it back without making any noise, not wanting to awaken the house; then with trepidation repeated the same operation on the other column. A small cylinder of flowered cardboard fell on the floor with a thud and rolled away.

He followed it, breathing heavily, among the hulking shadows of the furniture without daring to touch it. Finally he picked it up, kissed it, and holding it to his chest carried it to his writing table, where he opened it under the lamp. Inserting two fingers into the open end of the tube, he drew out the contents and unrolled them. Letters, letters, all on pale violet paper, all in a refined, cursive script, undoubtedly a man's handwriting but not his father's. At the top of one page he read "Elena! Elena!" and mentally translated this invocation into his own language; biting his lips, he murmured "Mamma! Mamma!" He realized he was forbidden to read the dates and signature and held the paper in his extended hands, far from his eyes, in a seeming effort to be myopic and not recognize the words. But words of love lit up for him at intervals under the lamp, like gleaming foam on the waves of the sea at night. He had a horror of reading them and was terrified of falling into temptation.

The electric light went out. The room was completely dark; nothing could be seen outside the shutters but a chaotic grayness. "Thank God," he murmured in the providential darkness, but that did not stop him from fumbling in his pockets for a match and lighting a candle. The dry, crooked wick crackled and gave off sparks before igniting.

Then he seemed to hear the voice of his dying mother begging: "Burn." And a tormenting image from his adolescence passed through his memory.

They were at the seashore. Famished after his swim, he had run, almost flown, to his mother's bathing hut, where he knew he'd find his afternoon snack on the white wooden table. Arriving at a run and intent only on entering the unoccupied hut, he pushed on the doorknob too forcefully and sprang the flimsy bolt inside. His mother was there in the room. He was at the avid age at which all women seem beautiful. What he saw of his mother—in a split second—was that waxen, dismal, and *dead* pallor that we see in the flesh where our own blood runs. He slammed the door shut and ran away, his clenched fists over his eyes. He was stricken by remorse, by the shame of having "seen" his mother.

Now, many years later, he was kneeling before the spent fireplace. In his left hand he held the bundle of letters, his mother's naked heart. Slowly he applied the candle flame to the paper. The words of love were consumed.

How strong must this passion have been if his

mother, who had even foreseen her sudden death, had always put off destroying the evidence? And was this, this discovery that had destroyed his mother's sanctity, the new misfortune he had been dreading for months? Again there rose before his eyes the enigmatic and disappointed figure of his father; a devious shadow crossed the gloom, that of the "other man," whom perhaps his father had known.

"It's not true!" he said, getting up and shaking off worse thoughts. "It can't be true. It must be a hallucination, a fever. Nothing, Mamma! Nothing!" he repeated in a low voice, in the hope of believing it.

He screwed the column back in place. He went to the fireplace and with his hand raked over the remains of the burned letters, concealing the charred and fragile bits as best he could under the andirons. It seemed to him there were no visible traces left.

Then the electric light came back on.

"No!" he almost cried out. And, having switched it off, he tiptoed toward the bedroom, his eyes wide open in the darkness, in search of sleep and impossible oblivion.

Elvira

Her husband having left her alone for three days in the hotel, Elvira felt physically numbed by her sudden freedom, like the proverbial little bird born in a cage who sees that the door is open and would rather not stay but doesn't trust its wings. For the first time, perhaps, she found herself face-to-face with herself. All that chatter of girlfriends in boarding school! All those brothers and little sisters and servants and housekeepers in her father's house! Then heedlessly she had got married, and the wedding had seemed to her prosaic and somehow painful—yes, even painful—like having to move to a new house. No honeymoon trip, just a hotel on the Italian Riviera, buzzing with the "right" people; and then, immediately thereafter, arrival at their so-called bridal home, no less densely populated than her father's, chock-full of ancestors and collateral relatives, overrun with political and professional friends who sat heavily at the long dinner table and crisscrossed it with conversations as discordant as the clatter of dishes. These customs were called patriarchal by her in-laws. Sometimes she got overexcited talking in competition with the others, but more often her mind wandered, and she felt her long shining eyelashes droop and her eyelids blink, seemingly wounded by too much light and too many voices.

It took two years and the death of her father before her husband could bring himself to take her along on a fortnight's trip; and a few evenings later, he received a telephone call and had to leave her. It made her truly unhappy.

"Come back soon, Duccio," she told him in all sincerity. "I'm scared to be alone."

When she awoke in the morning, she was surprised not to hear beside her the breathing of this man who was so close to her and yet so distant. She ran in bare feet to make sure the door was properly locked, then went back to sleep and began to dream a long baroque dream, like a novel in installments, interrupted by the bells and voices of the neighbors, which made her jump up with the impression that they were about to invade the room. Finally she had to wake up for good and realize that she hadn't succeeded in dispelling (not that she really wanted to) the thought that had been fixed in her mind since the day after their arrival: Speri is here, in this same city, in that other big hotel ten minutes away.

They had run into each other by chance on a deserted path in the park and had strolled together.

She, without thinking, had taken off a glove, and they had held hands. They had not exchanged more than a few words. But, even before this encounter, which in the absence of her husband seemed full of meaning, there had been little talk between the two and almost no interaction: an automobile drive, seven years before, during which the young pair, seated side by side, had felt too close; a long gaze; a few letters that anybody could have read but which Elvira alone thought she understood; a few entreaties from her that he find a way to see her, which Speri had either resisted out of laziness or submitted to without caring. There were hundreds of kilometers between them, the opportunities were rare, and he had deliberately let them slip. All during her engagement she had stopped writing him but resumed shortly after the wedding. And by and large they were the same insignificant words as before, which anyone, and her husband in particular, could have read, but now they concealed a different state of mind. She talked to him in her heart, recognizing in this man, so superficially close and so ungiving of himself, the one person in the world in whom she could confide; time and distance had made him more intimate. Indeed, she turned to him in her thoughts whenever she floundered amid the crowd that was crushing her life; and in that uncertain memory, that vague hope, she sought a little silence.

Now in the hotel, home to everyone, shut in with a lot of strangers who seemed to her hostile, she was truly afraid of being alone, and as though calling for help, she seized the telephone receiver; before she knew what she was doing, she had spoken the name of Speri's hotel and heard the number of the room he occupied.

"Speri," she said in a flat, detached voice. "Is it you? Good morning!"

He returned her greeting.

"My husband is away," she added. But there was no response. "Might we see each other?"

"Today?" Speri asked in his turn. "Let me think. I guess not. Lawyers and the notary for the whole day. It's no fun. As you know, I'm here for my sister."

Yes, she knew. It was perhaps the only thing he had talked about when they had met in the park. He was here to help his widowed sister disentangle certain matters of the inheritance that she found too difficult. And leaving the park, he had indicated with his gaze a young woman dressed in mourning approaching from a doorway and had said good-bye to Elvira with the words "There's my sister. I was on my way to meet her."

On the telephone, she became upset, insisting, "For the whole day? Not even an hour? What about this evening?"

"This evening?" he said while she marveled at having been so bold. "I've promised to take her to the theater."

"Isn't she in mourning?"

"Of course she's in mourning. Does that mean she has to die too?"

"Where are you going?"

He named the theater.

"Are you meeting her there?"

"I'm meeting her beforehand. We're to have supper together."

There was a pause during which neither of them found anything to say. Then she said, "So good-bye." And she started combing her hair in front of the mirror. She did not recognize her childish face.

"Passion!" she said to herself. "It makes us so ugly!"

And with her fingers laced around one knee and her eyes wandering, she realized she had spoken the word "passion."

She stayed in the room all day, reading a book, and had her meals sent up. But when it was almost evening, she went out, and her feet led her to that same pathway in the park where she had met Speri. She wandered back and forth two or three times, always returning to the front of the sister's house, as though wanting to spy on her. Finally she saw her emerge and followed her at a distance along the same sidewalk toward the center of town.

The woman was slightly taller than she and not so thin, with lighter hair and complexion. Elvira scrutinized her every movement, making comparisons, judging her own clothing and meek demeanor against that serene haughtiness. She was dressed in mourning herself, in expensive fabrics and an Astrakhan mantle, and certainly she had spent just as much as the other woman. But suddenly she felt badly dressed, and it seemed to her that her black garments were unbearably funereal, while the other woman's body swam, so to speak, in the dark and shining folds of her fashionable outfit and her hat was daring and the sheer black stockings in which her steps sprang forward seemed to have been selected for their color not out of homage to a dead man but on a whim to counter the mode of champagne-colored legs.

She also had the feeling that she was walking too fast, and she made an anxious effort not to run, so as not to be noticed, but still not to remain so far behind as to lose sight of the other woman in the growing evening crowd on the sidewalk. The plane trees along the sidewalk were variously yellow and green and made halos and canopies under which the woman's figure changed as it proceeded; the glow of the streetlamps mingled with that of the dusk; the windows of the shops, lighting up one by one, cast rays that by combining with the other beams produced chimerical reflections around the woman. All of a sudden, and deliberately, as though it had been fixed in her mind ever since leaving her house, she stopped in front of a show window, and Elvira, overtaking her, looked her right in the face. It was the same strong, well-shaped face as her brother's; the same cold and secretive eyes; above the eyebrows one imagined the same smooth forehead. In her, Elvira, contemplating her stealthily as a superior being, loved her Speri; she loved, almost, all their kin, comparing them, with an admiration that contained even humiliation and rage, to the people among whom it was her fate to be born and remain— people who wore their hearts on their sleeves and thought out loud.

These others, to be sure, were selfish and cruel, but at least they had in their nature that bit of the unexpected and reserved, that bit of silence and mystery that alone can make life acceptable, at least to a woman like herself, who had found none of it in her life except by reading a few novels she hid under her pillow. Thus did Elvira think, or feel, again following ten paces behind the unknown woman, who, her suspicions instinctively aroused, turned no less deliberately than when she had stopped in front of the show window and peered back. Elvira hid herself in the crowd and watched her disappear. She saw her walk into the center of the city, among men and rivals, at a slower pace, with the replete and knowing rhythm of women born to please.

The sister of the man she loved appeared to her as a woman of easy virtue. And this upset her. Now, five minutes from Speri's hotel, she turned and fled back to her own.

She went to bed trembling with cold and solitude. Where was Duccio, who would talk to her about everything impetuously, neither more nor less the way he would have spoken with a colleague or a young office clerk, to the point where she'd say to him, "Duccio, you're giving me a headache"?

This was a vigil, like the one before entering boarding school or the one before her wedding, and, as in all the other vigils, there was nothing in her heart but disorder and darkness. To put out the light, to sleep—and then? Later, when she awoke, she thought for a moment that she had only dreamt it, but the minute she was on her feet she ran to the telephone.

"Speri," she said in the same voice as yesterday. "Today too?" He unfurled his whole program for the day. He really hadn't the time. Tomorrow he expected to be freer.

"How about right after lunch? Busy?" And she raised her voice. No, not even right after lunch. He had to stay in the hotel and work. Things that couldn't be postponed. "With your sister?" "No sister." And it was clear that in replying this way he had smiled.

So she made up her face as best she could. But was not her beauty, if it existed, that of a restless child? And she despised it and found it faded. When the time came, and having eaten nothing, she went to the other hotel; she felt that whether it was inspiration or fate, it was all the same, for good or evil. She had the feeling she wasn't walking but that the pavement was moving under her feet and carrying her along.

Only when she faced the desk clerk did she come to herself. He was bearded and fattish; his rounded chest protruded from behind the counter. She gave the name of the man she had come to see.

"Call room forty-seven," he told a bellhop. "Show the lady to the lounge."

"I'm his sister," said Elvira firmly, without turning around, and darted up the stairs.

On the landing she encountered her own image reflected in an oval mirror topped by small Louis XVI coronets. And she scarcely recognized her distorted features, her mouth livid with lipstick.

"Ugly!" she said to herself. And the memory of the beautiful sister passed before her eyes. She wanted to go back, but she was afraid of how the desk clerk would look at her and what he might say.

So she started up the stairs again, breathless, already contrite before sinning, spoiled before having been plucked.

The Good Lady

Stori lived during the summer at Vico Alto, above the
Terme di Vico. Mornings he went down to the spa;
afternoons he received his patients up above, where
they arrived by the funicular. Guidi made the ascent in
the middle of August. Olive trees writhed on both sides
of the funicular, and it seemed impossible to him that
they didn't suffer.

Then, when he had reached the top, there was the
empty square sweltering in the sun, the sudden cool-
ness of the vestibule of Stori's villa, the dark anteroom.
The shutters were closed, the curtains drawn; the ticking of the pendulum clock traversed the room in all
directions seeming to measure it in paces. He knew he
had climbed a short flight of steps and had even counted them, nine; but he felt instead that he'd descended
into a catacomb. The servant who had opened the

door, which was painted black, to this waiting room, he too dressed in black, had disappeared like a ghost, and Guidi's own deep breathing, while his pupils dilated in the darkness, told him there was no one else there.

Though in the grip of inertia, he couldn't stand still and went searching for the farthest armchair. But sitting there in a feathered hat and with a huge stomach and a flabby red face that in the semidarkness looked almost phosphorescent was a woman patient; and he felt frightened, as though she'd been there waiting for him goodness knows how long. She glared at him. He drew back and found a seat near a window, where he leafed through an old hunting magazine full of pictures of dogs. Little by little the colors of the photos became visible to him, but he still had the impression that his eyes were wide open in alarm, with dark circles under them, in the painful effort to distinguish a furtive danger in the dim light. Then he fixed his eyes on a color plate showing a vigorous white beast, a large animal with a curled tail and pointed muzzle; and he kept looking at it expecting from one moment to the next to see the panting of its peony-colored tongue and the quiver of its receding flanks. That was how his health seemed to him, and he would almost have liked to become such an animal, greedy for its food, eager to run, happy to hear its own voice. And he dozed off, dreaming of fresh meadows in the moonlight and the yelping of invisible dogs.

He did not hear when the woman went into the doctor's office or when she left. He awoke suddenly to the voice of the servant calling him—"Signor Guidi!"—

a voice that sounded to him authoritative and yet tremulous, like someone unwillingly inviting him to an unavoidable torture. Then he quickly shook off that momentary well-being, that impression familiar to patients in a doctor's waiting room of being already cured, of having come for nothing; and all his unhappiness rose up to choke him.

Uncertain, with a sense of shame and guilt, he stepped into the consulting room. Stori stood before him, tired and attentive.

But why should everything in this place, where one went in search of health, be so gloomy? There was, to be sure, more light in the doctor's office; but the black leather of the seats and the examination table in the middle of the room, the black frame of a mediocre painting, even the black casing of the desk clock, imparted, especially in contrast with the white linen, a mournful emphasis.

And Stori himself: that face that looked like a mound of chilly clay, more or less patched together, the hair vaguely streaked with gray, and eyes that didn't match, one larger than the other, with the larger one round and protuberant, like a cold, precise optical instrument! Actually he had a good reputation; they said his family life was unhappy, his own health was known to be poor, but this made him better able to treat the ills of others, or at any rate to sympathize.

He made only a slight nod of assent when told the name of Guidi's family doctor, who had advised him to seek this consultation and persuaded him to make the journey. Guidi, exaggerating the absentminded acknowledgment of the recommendation, thought:

Why should I need to tell him who gave me his name—a name famous in Italy and abroad? He's not going to sell me health cut rate just to please my family doctor! Whereupon he got mixed up and rushed through his story. Confusedly, in a husky voice and pathetic tones, often running his fingers through his hair, he told of the torments of an exhausted man, a young man of thirty worn out by anxiety, who had rotted before becoming ripe, an unhappy man walking "on the razor's edge" and feeling vertigo at every step: the nightmares, the reawakenings in the dark, the sudden phobias, the longing to escape, the feverish exhaustion, the throbbing headaches at the temples, the obsessions, the horror of madness, the lure of suicide.

But the more carried away he got, the more the other appeared calm and impassive, paying only habitual attention, with neither curiosity nor effort. You might have said the family doctor had written him from Milan and told him the whole story. But no, it was obvious that Stori had heard it all a hundred times, and now his one concern was to guess the next sentence and mentally fit the confused story into the clinical framework, with its proper terminology and concise list of symptoms. Guidi felt a chill. No doubt he would shortly hear the same verdict pronounced once again: nervous exhaustion, real sufferings and imaginary illness—hence nothing to be done. The hope with which he had come to Vico collapsed, and it was his last hope: to hear that his illness was here or there but not something everywhere and nowhere, impossible to pin down, inevitable, surrounding his life like air and destiny; here or there, a tumor, a foreign body, some infection to be pinched between the fingers or eradicated with the scalpel or at least something you could die of! Instead, nothing—nothing and everything: destiny.

The story, stifled by Stori's silence, petered out and ended. The doctor had the patient lie down and unbutton his shirt and trousers; he palpated him, auscultated him, turned him over, applied pressure to his stomach, made him take deep slow breaths, asked him to repeat the ridiculous number thirty-three, examined his knee and pupil reflexes, and allowed him to stand up and get dressed. Then came the pronouncement: He was not to worry, he was to have faith; there was no cancer or progressive paralysis. While Stori, stepping away to his desk, prepared to jot down the usual prescriptions for powders and capsules, Guidi, with bated breath, awaited the odious words. These came too, all the more irritating since they were foreseen, and fell on him like whiplashes on a back already bowed: "Nervous exhaustion, that's all." They made him quiver and rock back on his heels, almost with an impulse to seize this man by the throat.

Now a dialogue of questions and answers ensued between the doctor at his desk and the patient standing at a distance. He lived in Milan? Yes, in Milan. What part of the city? Perhaps the noisiest, most congested part. Profession? Stockbroker. Married? Yes. For how long? Exactly three years and two months. Children? No. Did he go out in the evening—parties, social events, theater? Yes, of course; he went with his wife. There were intimate questions as well. Guidi was embarrassed. He answered briefly and spoke ill only of himself.

He must change his life, at least for a while, and

immediately. Diet, moderation, silence, and solitude were indispensable for the next two or three months. Neither seashore nor high mountains; hills, four or five hundred meters high, were preferable; the lake region excellent. Rest, walks gradually increasing in length, fresh air.

"Doctor," said Guidi, "I cannot rest. My financial situation hangs in the balance. Give me stimulants, strychnine, whatever you like, but don't tell me to stop. I can't do it. I can't go away. Even a two-day trip, this trip, is a disaster. I'm like a mountain climber who's reached a point where he can neither stop nor go back. He has to keep climbing to find his way. I can't help it, I have to keep climbing. Once I stop I'm lost."

"You're not lost," replied Stori. "You may get lost if you go on like this. You must stop and, if necessary, go back down a little."

"My wife . . ." faltered Guidi, and was about to continue.

But the sound of these words suggested to the doctor another piece of advice. Husband and wife, at least for the time being, ought to sleep in separate bedrooms.

Gasping as under a cold shower, his head forward and a hand outstretched, Guidi listened.

Then Stori spoke the words that determined his patient's life.

"Your good lady"—that was how he put it—"will understand. Your good lady will be able to help you recover."

"My good lady!" Guidi burst out. And he took two steps forward.

The doctor raised his left arm to his face, as though warding off a blow.

His good lady!

He saw her there in his mind as though she were present: fashionably thin with the narrow profile of an eaglet, a nose like a short knife blade, murky and enticing eyes, smooth bobbed hair dark as night, and a voice either shrill or hoarse. When he held her on his knees and felt her ribs under the cloth of her *toilette* and the silk of her blouse sticking to her flesh, he could feel her quiver like a famished beast. Her perfume dissolved in the smell of her hair. When he kissed her, there was not a feature of her face that did not decompose; he had the impression that her lips were swelling and that her makeup had darkened and was almost flaking off her cheeks like overheated paint. They had been married for a little over three years, and perhaps not a week went by without her saying "You go your way, I'll go mine!" and slamming the door in his face. One out of three times when they came home from a party, she, beside herself with fury, kept him in the doghouse for at least forty-eight hours, either because some woman had been wearing a more attractive outfit than hers or because he'd made a remark about the way she danced. Her way of dancing today's dances! Is there any other way of dancing today's dances?

"My good lady!" he cried, lunging at the desk a second time. "Why do you say that? What do you know about her? And . . . if only you knew! 'Your good lady!' That's what you say to all your married patients.

You talk like a fortune-teller, like a gypsy woman at a fair. There's no lucky planet. What do you know about my wife? A bitch! You know as much about my spleen and my guts. My wife is a devil and you're a charlatan."

"You're a madman!" said Stori, rising to his feet and trembling.

Guidi saw only his round and protuberant eye, like that of a Cyclops.

"Ha-ha," he laughed. "So I'm crazy! You've figured that out? The famous miracle worker has finally figured something out!" And seizing the prescriptions, he crumpled them into two balls of paper. "What do I owe you for the diagnosis?"

"Nothing," replied Stori, and rang the bell to call for help.

"Nothing! Everything!" yelled Guidi, scattering all the money he had on the desk, the floor, everywhere. Then, as the servant came in, he retrieved three one-hundred-lira bills and put them in his pocket.

"I'm taking these back," he said. "I'll need them for the trip."

He left like the wind, even forgetting his hat. People on the funicular drew away from him.

He ran to the railway station as though he were being pursued. He knocked with his knuckles on the ticket window. "Mombello. First class," he demanded.

"Laveno Mombello?" asked the clerk, leafing through the schedule.

"Mombello Madhouse!" he shrieked.

Now he was surrounded by a few people, then many, and they were convinced he was right. Two carabinieri placed themselves on either side of him, and when the formalities were over, he was put on the train with an escort. Stori had supplied the particulars of the case and returned the money. A carefully worded telegram was sent to inform his wife.

Once on his way, with the olive trees outside the train window fading in the evening, Guidi felt blessed and truly at ease. He'd had no more cause to argue with the ticket seller; he didn't even have to bother showing his ticket to the conductor.

Oil

While his wife was still alive, Calùmi had a country house halfway up the side of a hill. Those who know him and remember the lady can imagine the villa even without having ever seen it: not many rooms but large ones, polished floors, a veranda with columns, wide conspicuous gutters on the plain facade. That was just how they had found it, an old farmhouse; they had renovated it at little expense, but it looked made to order.

She especially was like this: lucid, a little cold, with the smooth forehead of an Umbrian Madonna. In former days, she had enjoyed wearing large hats with ostrich plumes or the straw hats of Florence. He, between thirty and forty years old, had attacks of unrequited youth, outbursts of enthusiasm or rage, short volleys of words, momentary as a hailstorm. The house resounded with them; she, the wife, listened; then the silence came back.

And for many months of the year they were enveloped by it on all sides and asked for nothing more, ever since Calùmi, almost without realizing it, had changed and accepted as good whatever seemed good to his wife, beginning with solitude. In addition to the house with its facade always in the sun, the good things in this place included the orchard, the thriving vegetable garden, the pond with water lilies, and the grove of oaks and maples through which a brook flowed. So everything was good—except for the sharp narrow angle made by the property uphill and to the right of the house. The gate was visible from the veranda, where when the weather was nice they ate; and between the bars of the gate and the sprays of wisteria you could see the path leading up from the roadway to the ten houses of Matusia at the top of the hill. Not that there were all that many passersby or that they were nosy. But it was annoying to think that it was their choice whether to keep going, as in fact they did, or to stop and peer or even to sit down right there.

Twice a day, at set hours, Uncle Gervasio went by. But from him there was really nothing to fear. He came down the slope from his shack, which lay behind four rows of American grapevines and alongside two fig trees; he went back up to his shack. As he approached you heard the cautious tapping of his cane on the stones; then he appeared, fairly tall but no more so than the cane, which he held like a crosier. Especially on his way down he resembled a poor saint carried in a procession, though no one had ever been seen walking beside him. He stared fixedly, if he was staring, straight ahead; he turned neither to one side nor the other. Slowly he measured each step, paying close attention to the sound of the cane as to the voice of a guide. His mouth, amid the few hairs of his scanty white beard, he kept slightly open, and though he breathed heavily, he didn't sound out of breath.

Whenever Calùmi's wife caught sight of him, she ran to the gate, more solicitous than she generally was. She greeted him anxiously: "Uncle Gervasio, how are you?"

It took the old man a moment, more than the blink of an eye, to emerge from his seeming daze and realize that there was actually someone in the world, just two steps away, who was concerned about him. Then he felt gratified; he turned to the woman benevolently but without smiling and, resting his swollen, yellowish hand on his staff, enjoyed being able to pause for a moment without admitting defeat.

"I'm fine, Signora. Just fine. I eat, I digest, I sleep—I get along all right. It's just my legs that don't want to hold up."

"Eh, what can we do about it? Eighty years old. . . . You know, you're not doing so badly; you look better than you did last year."

"Eighty-one, dear lady," he corrected her with mild pride and traced the two figures with his fingers. "Eighty-one on the Immacolata."

Then he continued on his way. With his little pot-belly acting as a counterweight, he held his shoulders straight. The tapping of his cane on the stones died away at the curve.

The acacias still had some green, but the maples were losing their leaves. The Immacolata, the Feast of the Immaculate Conception, was only a month away; immaculate snow would soon fall on the mountains.

Calùmi had been at Matusia for years without knowing much about Uncle Gervasio's life. His wife happened to tell him about it one autumn evening, shortly after the old man had gone by. He had known only that he was the uncle of the rich peasants from whom he had bought his house and land, and they still owned the fine farm to the left of his property. The uncle too owned a little plot of land; but his knees were wobbly—Calùmi, of course, knew this—and his arms were no longer strong enough to wield a spade, which meant he had allowed the space in front of the couple's house, the one you could see through the gate, to go to seed, and the scanty grass was mottled here and there with patches of red-violet clover. From time to time he too greeted the old man and got the same reply: "I eat, I digest, I get along all right. It's just that my legs don't want to hold up."

Now he learned that Uncle Gervasio certainly didn't live on four rows of grapevines, two fig trees, and an orchard about the size of a pocket handkerchief, but on a small annuity. If you could call that living! Before the war three lire a day had been sound gold lire; now they were paper or base metal alloys. He was alone all day long; he himself cleaned his bedroom and kitchen, the two rooms in his shack; he made the bed and dusted the crucifix. And so went the morning. Then he started preparing his food: a tureen of soup that he let cool and divided into two portions for his noonday and evening meals; a bowl of raw chicory or string beans or dried beans, depending on the season; sometimes, as a special treat, he cooked spaghetti. To hear the rumbling of the pot was (as he himself put it) a consolation.

Calùmi's wife told him these things.

"Just think! He goes all by himself with a jug to get water from the brook. He's put down a plank. And the plank wobbles! More than once he's fallen facedown with his hands in the water. He's never hurt himself seriously. He doesn't complain, he gets back up little by little; no one hears about it. . . . He likes his food, as well he might. . . . What he used to like most was good olive oil, when three lire were worth something. Now he can't afford it. He uses flaxseed oil on his salad, but he doesn't want it in the tomato sauce when he makes pasta. So he just squeezes the tomatoes, heats a little of the juice, and that's it."

Calùmi had stopped eating, and his eyes bulged. It was one of his moments for letting off steam.

"How awful! How awful!" he exclaimed. "What about the nephews? . . . Ah yes!" he remarked without waiting for a reply. "Nephews! Peasants. Landowners. Anyway, what does a family mean today? Wife and children. There's no more room for anyone else."

In the lamplight, the cruet full of olive oil that they ordered from Lucchesia shed a soft and feeble glow on the tablecloth.

"Send him a bottle of our oil!" cried Calùmi. "Right away! Tomorrow morning!"

"All right," his wife replied.

After thinking a moment, he went on, "Why don't we buy the land from him? Leaving him the use of the shack. That would give him some money. It would be a good deed. And there'd be some benefit for us. What do you think?"

"Is it worth it?" she asked.

In fact, it wasn't worth it; she was always right. Even if they paid a lot of money, people could say they'd taken advantage of a sick old man—that's what they'd surely say. And the nephews, who worked as gardeners on Calùmi's property and looked after the house when it was closed for the winter, the nephews, who were expecting to inherit from their uncle, would become enemies; the peace and quiet of Matusia would turn into secret war. It wasn't worth it.

"In fact," he concluded, "one ought to guard against expecting any benefit from a good deed. It means it's not good after all."

So they did nothing about it, except for the gift of oil—not a whole bottle but a nice little flask—which was delivered the next morning by their cook to the old man's cabin. Toward evening he stopped at the gate.

"Holy oil!" he said. "Holy oil!"

"What are you talking about, Uncle Gervasio?" the woman scolded him affectionately. "What are you talking about?"

"God bless you!" And he went on his way.

But a few days later he came by with a basket of Spanish figs and presented it to them.

"The last ones," he said. "The last of the year."

Then the Calùmis left for the city as they did every winter. They returned in April. When he saw Uncle Gervasio again, he asked his wife, "Have you started sending him the oil again?"

"I didn't think you meant forever. I thought it was just that once."

But he insisted. And from then on, every Saturday, the little flask of olive oil went up to the shack. And so it continued, and for the winter they left him three flasks.

"You're putting oil in the lamp," said the old man. "And the lamp doesn't want to go out."

"Eighty-five," he said one day, bidding them good-bye as they were leaving, and as usual tracing the two figures with his fingers. "Eighty-five on the Immacolata."

At the beginning of spring, Uncle Gervasio died. And he had made a will, designating as his sole heir "my benefactor Cavaliere Andrea Calùmi." Actually Calùmi had no such title, but that wasn't enough to invalidate the will.

"I'm sorry," said his wife when she found out. "We went too far."

But he wanted to accept, and this time he pre-vailed. How did they go too far? With some thirty or so flasks of olive oil? After all, they'd never had an ulte-rior motive, and the old man had acted spontaneously without ever letting on. There was no reason to behave as if they were afraid or had a guilty conscience. And besides, since they weren't members of his family, the inheritance taxes would exceed the price of the oil.

But what they had previously foreseen came to pass. The peasants became sullen and hostile. They went around saying how unfair it all was; that Uncle

Gervasio was a senile old fool, and the will wouldn't even be allowed to stand if the heirs were ordinary people; but these were arrogant city folks, and outsiders in Matusia took care to toe the line. Other faces darkened. How could you trust gardeners and caretakers, especially in winter? Enemies and hired hands. Calùmi, in his heart of hearts, was thinking that good and evil are closely knit and that nothing is so difficult as to do good without hurting the recipient, or others, and in the final analysis oneself. One should never go too far in anything, be always on one's guard, particular and sparing with one's feelings. And this conscientious man, walking and thinking, caught himself scratching his little pointed blond beard.

They had once thought vaguely of moving. Now they decided to sell immediately. Actually the additional land they had acquired, by eliminating that narrow angle and the need for the path, which with the commune's permission could be moved farther away, raised the price considerably, and this more than made up for what they had to pay in inheritance taxes.

One morning, by agreement, the purchasers, husband and wife, arrived. All four were on the veranda, along with one of the peasants, who was there to clarify some details about the upkeep. All of a sudden they saw smoke from the slope, and then flames.

"The oil!" cried Calùmi. Then, sniffing the air with quivering nostrils: "The oil has turned into kerosene!"

But his wife grasped his arm tightly to shut him up. Nothing but a few old boards and bricks. No point even calling the firemen, eight kilometers away.

"A bad omen!" said the new owner, watching the fire.

"Not at all!" said his wife, who was poetic. "The flames are beautiful, and it's just a hovel! To make a greenhouse out of it we'd have had to rebuild. This way we can start from scratch."

"And anyway," added her husband, "it's insured."

"I'm afraid not," said Calùmi. "Not the shack. I didn't have time. We'll deduct the value."

The two men went inside to talk it over. The new owner, who was not poetic, put a value of ten thousand lire on the shack and met no opposition. They came back out on the veranda.

Crackle and collapse. Flames shot up on the slope.

"Oil and kerosene!" Calùmi repeated, though his wife looked at him askance.

The peasant had caught the woman's look and gesture; he was well aware that they didn't want to be swamped by complaints and lawsuits. Cold and surly, with a touch of hoarseness in his opening words, he was emboldened to say, "Putting the kerosene was a dirty trick. But they were ill-gotten gains."

Ill-gotten gains! What gains are not ill gotten? So thought Calùmi, mocked by the flickering tongues of fire.

The Widower

Having sold their villa in the mountains, the Calùmis migrated to the seashore in search of more sun. But as with plants disinclined to put down new roots, the transplantation didn't take. Also they were followed to the sea by a dim feeling that their lives were pointless, unless the purpose of life is to contemplate life and to love one another in solitude. Today's world, however (we hear this said all the time), is not for contemplatives; and loving one another, without change, as regular as breathing, is like the clear sky and dead calm that can go on for months on the Mediterranean and may sometimes make you long for a storm.

Her character was the first to change. She became unsettled. She went so far as to talk about things on which, by tacit agreement, they had always kept strictly silent, even touching on the subject they'd avoided for so many years, fearing it would be cause for a lament—she spoke several times of the misfortune of not having had children. From time to time, especially on the finest days of summer, she gave vent to her sadness. She said they ought to take long trips, make their home in the city for good, adopt a little girl—it was all confused—but the point was to devote themselves to something, to devote themselves to life, to get out of themselves and go somewhere else. When life loses its stability, you get dizzy the first time you have to cross an empty space.

Thus it was that with her first illness, Signora Calùmi departed—forever. It was something incredible, devastating: a blast of sound in the silence, a clap of thunder when you can't tell what part of the sky it comes from. It took three days from the first signs of fever until the danger was apparent and three more until the end. Then a slamming of doors and shutters, footsteps on the stairs, the stamping of caparisoned horses at the gate, and that was all. Once they had taken her away, he stretched out his hand in the empty room and said "All right!" He said this in the contained and trembling voice of someone who acknowledges a blow and promises an answer when the time comes. On what did Calùmi want to take revenge? On fate, which they had always treated, so to speak, with kid gloves and which had repaid them with an iron fist? Husband and wife used to say: "One must deal politely with fate, delicately, prudently, and not provoke it. That way it goes by and pays you no mind." And now, uninvited, unprovoked, fate had gone by and torn them asunder.

But even more incredible than the sudden catastrophe after twelve motionless years with barely a few small vexations, a few moments of melancholy silence, more incredible than Lia Calùmi's death was the last evening of her life. She had never been expansive, had never liked dramatic gestures; her feelings, shrouded in modesty, could perhaps be guessed from a shadow, or a brightness, appearing on that sincere brow, but they did not seek expression in words.

Instead, that last evening she tried to grasp her husband's hand and said to him, like any other woman, "Andrea . . . Andrea . . . I ask you . . . I ask you . . . swear to me you won't marry someone else."

A shiver came over him. He hadn't thought she was aware that her condition was hopeless. He himself kept hoping for a miracle. So he longingly squeezed her hand, straining in a loud voice against the grief that was trying to break out: "Lia! Lia! What are you talking about? You're going to get well."

"I'm not going to get well," she insisted solemnly. "Swear to me."

But at that moment, a finger tapped at the door and the nun came back in; the sick woman struggled to turn her eyes from husband to nurse. He could no longer restrain himself and fled to his room to weep with his head in his hands. Perhaps his dying wife's absurd thought—that he might remarry—did not even pass through his mind. All he could think of was that his companion was leaving him.

He pulled himself together and went back to her. The nun stared at him. Lia's breathing filled the room. Now nothing was to be seen under her eyelids but a little white of the eye, flickering and watery. She did not regain consciousness and died during the night.

Thus she did not get her husband's promise. He was unable to speak until in the empty room he spoke those two words: "All right."

Accustomed to solitude, he could not avoid it even by moving to the city. Yes, the city, Rome, where he decided to live for fear of memories that for him were becoming ghosts. But he took a house all for himself on a remote side street off Via Nomentana: a white cube set among four dark umbrella pines. Actually city life itself appeared there as only a memory, a ghost; the plaster was too white and in the sunlight turned a dazzling blue; the pines too dark, like an isle of the dead. In the evening the clang of the tram, from the street not five hundred paces away, seemed to come from a fairy tale; the reflections of the streetlights, blurred by the trees and lost in the faint glimmer of a residential area, resembled the feeble illumination of a fair after all the people have left. Even at noon the bells sounded as though one were hearing them at sea.

He had relatives in Rome, as had his wife, friendly households from other times. He began paying calls. Even had he not been dressed in mourning, you would have guessed from something in his appearance and bearing that he was a widower, but he did not carry his desolation around with him and was not out of place in company. He was still young in years, and younger in looks, with fine teeth and only one false tooth, which gilded his smile a little too much. But the pointed blond beard, the jacket buttoned up at the waist, that flawless reserve, those same high spirits, rare, sudden, and immediately subdued, gave him the air of an elderly youth who had stepped out of a painting to join the living. There was silence when he entered a drawing room or left it; the young ladies, clustered in a corner, looked bewildered, as though they were trying to calculate his age and his income.

His wife's aunt, who had a nice marriageable daughter, one day put her hand on his, saying, "So sad! So alone! . . . When one has been loved. . . . But you're young, Andrea. Life can't be over for you, even if you wish it were!"

He adroitly disengaged his hand and soon took his leave.

There was a feeling of remorse that he kept in reserve. Warily, he avoided examining it, but he knew that at the proper moment he would find it intact and enlarged. Certainly it had not been out of cruelty that he had denied his wife the oath; his emotions had been too strong and had unhinged his mind; he had not wanted to confirm to the dying woman the certainty of her death. Then too there had been a grotesque hitch when the chance could no longer be recovered: returning to her room, he would have promised her anything but had not foreseen that he would find her in her death throes. But why had he not sealed her ear with that word, even if it were at the last moment? Instead he had remained silent, stifled by anguish, blindly convinced that she was no longer conscious. And perhaps she had died suffering a thousand times more than necessary, prey to jealousy, she who had always shown

contempt for that dark, low passion! Then having started down such a slippery slope, he began to suspect that
there might have been in him, unknown to himself, a
certain touch of egoism, a repugnance, let's say, for
final promises, or even what might be called an instinc-
tive result of that fastidious and empty habit of not
tempting fate. When late in the evening such thoughts
assailed him in bed as he tried in vain to focus his
attention on the page of a book, he would put out the
light and with clenched fists, like a frightened child,
seek mercy in sleep.

Besides, the house was gray and untidy, expensive
and without even the cold distinction of luxury. Linen
maid, manservant, cook—and still the place was drea-
ry. When one has been accustomed since youth to a
woman's company, she becomes indispensable, even
when not kissing her. Her high voice, in counterpoint
to the lower tones of the man, is enough; the rustle of
her skirts; the fresh odor that comes in when she opens
a door, as though a window had been opened; the
thousand and one shining, useless things with which
she surrounds the monotony of the days like a tinge
of fleeting gold that embellishes the clouds at sunset.
She is a tinkle of words; the air one breathes; a more
fragile and delicate light, like the kind that passes
through lace.

And so it came about that to give orders to the servants and reduce expenses, or at least make them bear
fruit and not create a poor impression when a friend
was invited, to buy service that was not odious since
the old one had crumbled, and to vary those hotel
meals—it was for these and similar reasons, as well
as to rid the house of that air of a new second-class rail-

way coach that bachelors' homes have when they're well kept, that Mademoiselle Eugénie Leroux, an impeccable and attractive Frenchwoman of twenty-five, entered Calùmi's employ as a housekeeper.

One day when she was seated before him, with her nicely tapered leg exposed by her short skirt, and was charmingly explaining Proust's Odette to him, Calùmi all of a sudden no longer heard the words and felt instead a band of fire pressing on half his skull, from his temple to the nape of his neck. He leaned forward and put his arms around her waist.

"*Monsieur?*" she said with mild reproach. "*Monsieur? Qu'est-ce que vous . . . ?*"

He leaned backward on his chair. Now he could hear the ticking of his pocket watch.

"*Oh!*" the young lady went on. "*Vous m'avez fait peur.*"

But was that quiver of her cheek the sign of future wrinkles? And why did the light, striking the soft down, the blond *duvet,* make it look like a badly shaved beard? Up to this moment he had found her pretty.

And now? Wasn't she winking at him? Squinting, as though she had something in her eye?

"*Mon ami!*" she said and reached out to take his hand.

He stood up. "*Veuillez me pardonner. . . . J'ai eu tort.*"

And he walked out of the room.

Then the years went fast, the first years on the down-grade, those that retain the ardor of youth, but it is an ardor of abandon. You do the first stretch in a hurry, almost willingly, almost with the strength accumulated on the way up; you leave the summit behind, without turning to look back; farther down, you put on the brakes; another slope begins, a longer and more level one; and it is old age.

Outwardly Calùmi had not changed. At the club, at the theater, at parties, he was the same as ever; and young ladies no longer all that young had not lost interest in him. He felt changed within. And he had the strange feeling that others were aging in a hurry: the linen maid, the waiter, his wife's aunt. Then he smiled, realizing they were mirrors in which he was looking at himself.

So long as he was with other people he felt calm. When in the late evening he returned home, memories came forth to meet him in ever increasing swarms. At first he tried to drive them away, then stopped. Instead he began ransacking drawers and papers, putting in order and cataloging Lia's letters, locks of hair, photographs, snapshots. Sometimes he opened her perfume bottles, the last ones she had uncorked. Before going to bed he threw open the door to the balcony to air out the room. But nothing gave him pleasure at that hour. On rainy autumn nights he felt as though he were drowning in the rain; if it was clear, the twinkle of stars over the funereal pines pierced his heart.

One evening as he was closing the window, Lia almost visibly appeared to him. "Why did you let me die like that?" she said.

"I know," he replied under his breath. "I should have sworn to you not to marry anyone."

What had it been worth, that lifelong reserve of his, his sobriety of thoughts and words, the watchful care—whether it was astute or religious he couldn't say—not to challenge or tempt fate?

One by one, the women he might have married emerged from the shadows: Lia's cousin, his friend Ghezzi's sister, General Furnò's widow, Mademoiselle Eugénie Leroux. . . . Oh, the widow Furnò! That one made him laugh.

All together they filed past.

Any one of them!

He went back out on the balcony.

"I should have sworn not to get married again. But then to marry any one of them!"

He was astonished to hear, suspended in the air, the sound of the voice with which he had uttered these words.

He held in his hands—as he would have said—those two sentences, like the ends of a dry stick that he had broken on his knee: the dry stick of his life.

Hussàn-abà

He alone knew what my love had been for the woman I'll call Eleonora and of Eleonora's love for me. It was truly a consuming fire, the furthest you can imagine from adventure or caprice; we had thrown our youth into it, and even years later we did not dare to touch the ashes for fear of seeing the glowing red coals that our hearts had once been. There are things in my life that I cannot boast about, but this is one I am unable to regret, not the years I lived in a secret frenzy and not even the day when, almost on the spur of the moment, we agreed to separate. Our hands clasped, but standing upright, two people as distinct from each other as they could possibly be, we said farewell, knowing we thus wanted our love not to perish but to remain perfect in memory—something eternal. But there were no romantic leave-takings; from time to time I paid her a visit, and, alone or with a few other people, beside her splendid green marble fireplace, we discussed the issues of the day.

This love, truly unique for both of us, was so different from the usual ones that no one suspected it. We succeeded in living, as far as others were concerned, like beings invisible in a fog. She, a beautiful young widow, but rumored to be cold or chaste; I, free and a bachelor, but scarcely inclined to casual affairs—to people around us we did not seem made for each other, and without giving it a thought, they kept us forever apart even before we had actually met. Thus we were spared gossip for three terribly happy years, and later we could suffer at length without becoming ridiculous.

He alone, Murari, knew. But no one could resist Murari at certain times, especially in heart-to-heart conversations after midnight. Seated before me in my room, his face slightly forward, he listened and spoke. His eyes—and I've never seen others like them—his soft, deep, persuasive eyes dilated as though trying to take in the world. He knew everything about everyone. Rich and not ambitious, unmarried but not a libertine, his sole commitment (now that I understand him) was to a kind of seduction of souls, a hunt for secrets. His knowledge of so many mysteries gave him an enigmatic power, a fascination between that of the necromancer and the inquisitor that grew all the more the less he made use of it. When he glimpsed a secret, he threw out—this was often his method—a confidence of his own, perhaps an insignificant one, but in a strong, melodious, mysterious voice; then he made that incantatory play with his eyes, and the other person, unable to resist the bait, gave himself away completely and revealed his most intimate secrets. And Murari, clutching the secret, swallowing it almost physically (now that I understand him), felt a kind of jolt, as though he were satisfying his hunger. When I was constrained to tell him about my relations with Eleonora, I at first had the impression that I'd really told him nothing—or something he'd already known from the beginning, having been let in on it by the Holy Ghost. Then I was fearful, but he shook my hand, enclosing it completely with his long, dry fingers, and wordlessly, with only his gaze, said to me, "How can you doubt me?" If to me Eleonora was love, Murari was friendship.

How was it possible that he would one day betray me?

I had gone to see Eleonora toward dusk on a day in February—almost two years had passed since the day of our separation and it still felt like the eve—and there in the vestibule I recognized Murari's fur coat. There were no other visitors. He was sitting alongside the green marble fireplace, in which no wood was burning, and Eleonora sat facing him on a high leather chair. The light was dim and gloomy. I don't know why but we greeted one another awkwardly. There was a long silence.

Whereupon Murari began a perfidious play of the eyes. He gazed first at Eleonora, then at me, and then back at her. The conversation was sluggish, dull. I noticed, in the shadows, that Eleonora's fingers were trembling.

"What's the matter, Murari?" she said finally. "What are you staring at?"

"The light is so poor we can hardly see one another," he replied and laughed gaily. "This February is the color of mud."

"I'll leave you both for a moment," said Eleonora, rising.

"Am I in the way?" continued Murari, and turned his head slightly toward the departing woman.

We were left alone for more than a moment. I didn't dare say a word to him; I couldn't believe my eyes and ears and was afraid, or hoped, he'd gone mad, if only to have an explanation for what he'd said. He began to talk, acutely, dispassionately, suavely, about politics. But I wasn't listening.

Eleonora came back, squeezing in her hand a little cambric and lace handkerchief. First she flicked two switches, then turned one off again, giving the room a soft yellow light. She came to sit down and rejoin us, but she looked unsteady on her feet and seemed to quicken her steps in order to overcome it.

"Our friend," said Murari, "doesn't share our opinion."

"Ah, no?" she said, if only to say something.

Then Murari, with overelaborate affected precision, explained wherein our alleged disagreement lay. Eleonora meanwhile served tea. As she handed me the cup, she trembled so impulsively that some drops spilled on the carpet.

"Oh, Signora!" I cried. "I beg your pardon."

"It's nothing, never mind," she said in a dull voice.

Murari had paused and for too long remained silent. Then he went on talking about politics with order and accuracy; there was nothing he didn't know and understand. I grasped his thinking only marginally; but I couldn't say he was wrong, I could only hate him. When he had finished, no one had a word to say.

"Shall we go together?" he asked me in a friendly way after a pause.

"I don't know," I said.

But Eleonora remarked, "You don't live far from each other."

We both got up, first Murari, then I. She saw us to the door of the drawing room, saying "*Arrivederci! Arrivederci!*" in two different tones, as though her voice were breaking and she could no longer hold back her tears.

Once we were on the stairs, Murari drew closer to me and with deeply human concern (his dark eyes illuminated the shadows) asked, "But, my dear fellow, what's the matter? What's happened?" And he started to put his hand on my shoulder. "What's the matter?"

"I . . . I . . . ," I said, panting; and with the shoulder he was about to touch, I gave him a shove.

"You're crazy!" he said, drawing himself up and slightly quivering. "All right! You'll hear from me."

Two days later we fought. At the site, he came forward and stepped back with an air of forbearance, a resigned and weary manner that suggested he was taking this boring ceremony upon himself for the sole purpose of satisfying a friend's whim. He gazed at me indulgently, with paternal benevolence. He let himself be wounded. I didn't want to shake his hand. And I never saw him again. I saw Eleonora a few more times, but always less often. I was never able to explain things to her, and she always took care not to be alone with me. Anyway what was there to explain? Now I seem to see her standing on the other side of a broad, foggy river; I can hardly make her out; and the paths of our lives will never cross again.

I am unable to separate the memory of Murari from that of my big hunting dog, Hussàn-abà, a griffon I had for a summer and, after a year's interval, again until he died.

When I had him for the first time, I took him in as virtually a stray. My neighbors, having fallen overnight—one might say—into poverty and being forced to move out with desperate haste, would have abandoned or drowned him; they had no time to sell him properly. By buying him for a couple of hundred-lira bills, I saved him at the last minute from death or mistreatment at the hands of the first lout who might have got hold of him.

He had the fleece of a sheep and the hot, glowing palate of a wild beast. His ears were humble and dangling; his eyes, tender and modest, I'd say almost devoted—one could not imagine those of a slave girl to be softer—with a velvety darkness in which sulfurous sparks glinted and where I seemed to divine more than a dawning of human intelligence and a docile despair, almost an appeal for an impossible rescue. But when he opened his mouth, you saw, amid that stringy beard, teeth as long and sharp as daggers sprouting from the wet gums. His round, black nostrils looked like the two openings of a double-barreled shotgun.

I didn't even ask what his first owners had called him. I named him Hussàn-abà, with a sound vaguely imitating the gasping and eager panting of his breath when he ran. He rarely barked; he repressed it himself, stopping at the first outburst if his voice—shrill and hoarse at the same time—threatened to explode.

If I'd left him at home, I called "Hussàn-abà!" when I came back. The tufts of his whitish-brown fur fluttered as he ran; his impatient breath came near like a rising hot wind; his eyes were like two approaching lamps.

"Hussàn!" I repeated, sitting down. He put two paws on my shoulders, covering me completely, almost embracing me.

"Abà!" I panted, which made him excited. He put his paws on my head and opened his mouth; he blew the fumes of his strength on my face.

One evening while I playfully struggled, the paws somehow lost their grip on my head, scraped downward, and his claws scratched my temple.

"Abà!" I yelled, meaning perhaps to scold him. He planted his paws on my hip, ripped the cloth from my shoulder with his teeth, and, snarling, drew blood. I repulsed him, almost throttling him; kicking him in the belly, I drove him out of the house. I never wanted to see him again. It was already night. The next day I left for the city.

But I returned to those parts, to the same villa, the following year. One rainy evening I was on my way home, alone as always; I could not hear my own footsteps on the now deep and sticky mud. All of a sudden I heard behind me a patter of swifter and even more silent feet; I turned around anxiously, just in time to glimpse a gray form in the last flickering gray light; then drenched woolly fur rubbed against my knee.

I remember a firefly glimmering in a hedge. I took Hussàn-abà back. His damp melancholy eyes gave no inkling of how he had lived during that year.

Undignified as it may be, I confess I wept when he died.

I remember that firefly in the hedge, and I remember the odor of his poor flesh, his panting breath the same as when he bit me.

I cannot think that Hussàn-abà, my big hunting dog, was savage. In a dark impulse, a burst of strength, he "had" to hurt me.

And so, much as I'd like to think otherwise, the same goes for Murari, my Carlo, and what for me was friendship. In a burst of strength, and an excess of intelligence, he "had" to make me suffer. It was that need to live that, when carried away, almost necessarily turns cruel.

I've sought to be free and pure. And I'm convinced that all sentiment is passion and that reason counts for nothing. I separated from Eleonora so that love would remain pure and perfect, and I lost her forever.

I've had other friends since Carlo Murari, more loyal and dependable ones. But none to equal him.

Perhaps, one autumn evening on some street corner, I'm to meet him again. His head slightly tilted, he'll look at me, dilating those eyes whose like I've not seen since. I will take him by the arm.

Eureka

That Argia's lost letters no longer had much importance he, her brother Pietro, knew very well. No one
could awaken her from where she lay underground or
force her to hear those documents read and to recognize, frankly, that she'd been wrong to kill herself. And
people, people themselves, even the most malicious,
were not asking for explanations; for the dead go by in
a hurry, and when someone has done something crazy,
everyone is ready to boast of having known all along
that he or she had always been like that.

Yet Pietro, four nights after his sister's suicide, began looking for those missing letters, and he wouldn't
give up. He refused to give up until he'd found them,
and he was sure he would. And when his wife fearfully
put a hand on his shoulder, saying "Forget about it.
What does it matter to you?" he replied, "The letters

don't matter. I know that. What matters to me is finding them, that's all. It's the principle of the thing."

Then slowly she withdrew, tiptoeing away so as not to make the parquet floor creak; she left him alone, among piles of paper pulled from drawers and gaping files, with all the lamps lit in the empty summer night. And from the doorway she said, "Good night, Pietro," in a tone that expressed the pain in her heart.

There were three letters to be found, collected in a yellow envelope. How different they were in appearance! One was an almost stylish, ivory-colored card; another a small sheet of stiff blue paper; the third and last jotted down, with underlinings and blots, on a page of graph paper ripped from a notebook. But so similar in content! Three times in the course of months and years Argia had felt the need to confess, and each time she had written the same things, but each time in a more vehement tone, more emphatically inspired. "Don't think," she had written him, "that I don't know myself, that I don't know who I am. Even my religious mania . . . nothing but a mania, a poison. Maybe all the bad blood of our family has collected in my veins, unfortunate me, who might have hoped to be happy as long as I could hope to have you share my unhappiness. Now you've got married, and you and your wife tolerate me in the house, but I can't love her, it's not her fault, but she's too different from me, and she has you all to herself. There's no room for the sister. You two have to live; I have to die, disappear, and your consciences needn't trouble you. You won't find me when you come back, and you can forget about me, because it was all my fault."

Instead they had come back from their trip and there she was in the house, thin, taciturn, her dark eyes radiant, mumbling prayers even between one mouthful and another when they were seated at the table, spying on their love, the very looks they exchanged, as if they were sins of perdition. A ghost!

And she herself, like a ghost, had brought him the third letter, the one on the scrap of graph paper, one summer night while he, his back to the door, was working at his desk. He heard the door open behind him and thought he perceived in a warm breeze the fragrance and rustle of his wife, and, without turning around, waiting for her to cover his eyes with her fingers, he said, "My love!"

"I'm not your love," Argia replied. "I'm . . . me!"

Her dark hair hung loose in a sad cloud. Handing him the letter, she fled. She had said "I'm me" as she might have said "I'm death." And it was of death that the letter spoke: "I feel that it's fate, fate that once before wanted a victim in our family, and that nothing can save me. But it won't happen in your house; you and Rosa must be happy; I'll go away and die alone. I beg you to let me go."

Then, all winter long, she never mentioned it again. In the spring she began to talk about her need for solitude, meditation, a retreat. She spoke calmly, almost unctuously, but at the end of the sentence her voice became rather strident. So Pietro did what he could to make the separation easier for her; he found her a small apartment and made financial arrangements so that she would be independent. She refused to let her sister-in-law help her pack her bags, but she kissed her in the doorway as she was leaving. Her brother took her to her new living quarters in a suburb on the edge of the green plain.

"Anything you need?" he asked.

"Nothing," she said.

"We'll be seeing you?"

"Shortly."

Shortly! Two weeks later she killed herself. She left a note: "My brother and sister-in-law did not want me with them. I want them to be happy. They shouldn't be bothered by the memory of me. I ask God to forgive me."

You might have thought such a person would die huddled beside a brazier of coals. Instead she had procured a small-caliber revolver, which had left a neat round little hole in her temple not much bigger than the ones punched in letters before they are filed away in binders.

Pietro had punched all three of her letters in this manner and had filed each in alphabetical and chronological order in its proper binder. But in the last month that Argia had been living with them he had thought of discussing the subject with her, letters in hand, to prove that the fault was hers and that she herself had acknowledged it in writing. So he had taken the three letters out of the three binders and put them in a yellow envelope to keep them handy. Then the opportunity for the discussion failed to materialize. What good are explanations anyway? And who was to judge? He was afraid of hatred and anger.

The fourth evening after his sister's death, he resolutely opened the drawer of the desk where he kept pending letters and failed to find the envelope. He began searching for it methodically, at first only at odd moments, then for whole evenings, and finally shutting himself up at home without doing anything else until he found it.

In his state of mind when he began the search he was looking for explanation and proof, as though there were a judge who required written evidence of his innocence or the ghost of Argia were demanding a reckoning and justice. But on this point his wife was able to dissuade him; and he soon saw clearly that there was no one, outside his own conscience, to whom he should or could show the lost letters. But where in his conscience did the feeling of innocence end, and where did doubt begin? Had he fully obeyed his mother's wish when she had entrusted that poor creature to his care? Yes, he had, for many years; but it had perhaps been imprudent to get married after many years of life as a brother without first separating himself from his sister. And he couldn't say he'd suffered when Argia had left, though he had concealed his sigh of relief even from his wife. And had not the very care he had taken to guard those "documents" been in preparation for an alibi?

He preferred not to think of these things. Nor did he want to think about madness, which, hidden in his family for two generations, had now once again made its appearance. From this area of his consciousness he kept aloof, as from a small, lethal deposit of explosives near which it was better not to strike a match.

And so, having acquired a shade of awareness, the search had become an end in itself. It was the principle of the thing, the countering of the invincible disorder of his papers, and thus of his life. Without doubt, he had a meticulous, even pedantic, love of order, but it was a passion that was constantly being defeated. For a while he would succeed; then he had only to fall behind by the end of the day and there came avalanches of papers to be reconsidered, and his correspondence piled up in drawers or in unexplored pigeonholes.

Still, he never threw anything away, and that envelope, which he had put in a secure—too secure—place and forgotten, had to be somewhere. Nobody could have stolen it. There were four cabinets in the study and two in the hallway. He opened and closed them and flipped through papers, which he tied up in bundles, checking off on a list each drawer as he searched it so as not to go back over the same route. He felt a dull well-being, a salutary fatigue, like someone who climbs a tortuous mountain path without seeing the summit but knows it is there. Except one evening he felt shaken and broke out in a cold sweat at the thought that this stubborn search was a wager with destiny, with life. If he found those letters, there was justice and order in the world; otherwise not. This dangerous thought came like a flash of lightning. But he extinguished it and began again with the same energy.

He wanted no help from his wife. "You just get in the way," he told her. She said to him, "They don't serve any purpose, but you'll find them." "Yes, yes," he answered and let her know that he preferred to be alone.

But the image of Argia as a little girl was always with him. And always before his eyes he had the ever more perfect vision of that envelope, a little crumpled on the right and at the top, bulging slightly in the middle, so substantial and every hour more so that even had it not existed, his imagination would have been able physically to create it. Being superstitious, he had never opened a small inlaid casket that he kept on the shelf of his writing desk. Only when all the other searches had proved futile would he plunge his hand inside it and with eyes shut tight draw out the envelope.

They were futile. A July night ended, a little before dawn. He closed up the last drawers and cabinets. Disheveled, his face burning, he went to the casket and shutting his eyes (which even saw the creases in the envelope!) put his hand inside. It was empty.

But he drew out his hand with the thumb and forefinger almost joined as if they held the documents suspended; and with the other hand he knocked so loudly on the wall that his wife woke up and came running.

"Eureka!" he cried, standing there motionless and holding out his fingers. "Eureka! I've found them."

"I told you you'd find them. So now we can go to the country and you can get some rest. . . . But what do you mean? Where are the letters?"

"Right here. Don't you see them? Eureka!"

The light was blinding.

He twitched his hand, in which he felt the weight of the imaginary letters, triumphant at having found them. A laugh of burned-out intelligence spread across his face.

She staggered, called his name aloud; she knelt to embrace his knees, drew back in horror, writhed on the floor. But he just stood there in the same position, and his laughter was blissful.

Lean Harvest

I'm no good at dissembling, and I don't like to be cruel; yet this is what happened to me that September in San Godenzo.

As soon as he recognized me, Filippi came bounding toward me, just as he used to. And he left his bride several paces behind.

"Hey, old man! You're up here too! And in September! What weather! What luck! What a surprise! It's been so long since we've seen each other! Years, eh? . . . Tecla!"

But Tecla, under a rowan tree festooned with scarlet clusters, scarcely budged. So I, preparing to bow and be introduced, said to my friend (but in a low and doubtful voice): "The young lady . . . your daughter?"

"Your daughter." That's what I said. And I was the first to be stunned by the sound of my own words and blushed before he did. As though it were possible, apart from the difference in age, for anyone seeing them for the first time to think so, he with gray hair that still showed traces of blond, and she with dark hair tinged with gold! To think that I, who had known Filippi since his early youth, single and alone, and who had only lost sight of him in the last five or six years, could attribute to him a daughter, even one in early youth! A touch of malice had flashed through my habitually polite temperament, like lightning in a clear sky.

He wasn't thunderstruck, but he wavered. Still, he put a good face on it and, having pulled himself together, reacted with the casualness required by convention in such circumstances.

"Tecla! My daughter! Listen to him! What a way to call me an old codger! May I present my wife"—with a little tremor of emotion he took her gently by the hand and blissfully uttered her name and surname—"Tecla Filippi. But you're not my daughter," he said jokingly, pushing her away.

She laughed, a long rippling, bubbling laugh, which made you think of her soft hidden throat. How beautiful she was! And more than beautiful—for not everything about her was of classical perfection, and her lips, the lobes of her ears, even her nostrils, were somehow too full—how pleasing! If only we were able to pronounce this tired word with the gusto of that Spaniard who called his mistress Placerdemivida. There was not one of her movements, nor highlight on her face, that was not warm and living. Even when she had stopped laughing, she still sparkled a bit amid her strong perfume.

But his face darkened, and he became a little nervous.

"Didn't you get the announcement?" he asked.

I lied. Once you've started down the primrose path!

"That's right, you didn't answer." He commented on my denial with bowed head. "But it's strange! Whatever made you think . . . ? My daughter!" And again he gave a forced laugh.

We walked together toward the hotel. But a slight chill remained.

Sometimes, in the following days, I saw them walking ahead of me on the road but was unable to overtake them. No sooner had he glanced back and caught sight of me than he took her hand, left the road, and led her across the meadows; and, as happens in mountain meadows, especially in the September sunlight, the farther away they went, the bigger they looked.

Adorable Tecla! With her thirty-five-year-old beauty as constant, it seemed, as the clear sky of that September! With her delightful past as an almost backward child, living among dolls and illustrated books until the age of eighteen, then as a triumphant young belle at costume balls, who kept turning around to see how people were looking at her.

She was eighteen when Filippi, who was more than thirty and already somebody, asked for her hand. He literally asked for it on the spot, having said not a word either to her or to anyone else but presenting himself, hat in hand—which in those days was a black bowler—to her father and mother. Not wishing to give him a curt no, they took time to think it over, but they didn't mention it, either then or for some time thereafter, to their daughter. Anyway, when the time came, they told him no—Tecla was still too much a child. But the truth was that he was neither young enough nor rich enough; and he didn't even look healthy, with those little blue veins gleaming like enamel beneath his transparent skin.

They gave her to a rich young man, who died after a few years, years that for her were the primary school of love. In her long widowhood, of course, she learned more. Two lovers? Three? A decent number, and less than could be counted—even by the most malicious— on the fingers of one hand; not flirtations but something destined for her and for them; simple, almost forthright, almost acknowledged but without ostentation.

And then, when she should have begun to decline, Filippi came back into her life. Already you glimpsed the rosy tint of his skull, begonia pink, under the faded hair; some of the blue veins had also turned a delicate coral pink under the ever more diaphanous skin. And it was hard to understand why he didn't cut his mustache according to the fashion; it was full and strong but now white. His eyes were the same as before, restless but never distracted, timid and yet tenacious. Now he was more than somebody, and he was rich.

He waited for the right moment when she would be alone in the house. He sat down not too close to her and spoke at length of many things that he knew well, only rarely looking her in the eye. Odd that he always entered, and sat down, with his hat—which now was gray felt—in his gloved hands, and he never put it down. So that one day, while he was talking more fervently and crushing the felt brim between his fingers, Tecla said to him, "But, Filippi, why don't you ever put down your hat?"

"Will you permit me," he asked in a voice that had become intimate and resonant, "to hang it in the vestibule?"

"But, Filippi!" she cried, meaning to say, "Why should you even have to ask me such a thing?"

But the sight of his solemnity still imprinted on his face exhilarated her too much to be able to go on. Her speech was interrupted by her laughter, and her laughter went off like skyrockets, like Catherine wheels, in diatonic scales and syncopated trills, with heaven knows what sparkle of teeth and tints of orchid red in her throat, tilted back and gargling; until Filippi— Filippi!—had an attack of violence and seizing her by the shoulders with both gloved hands . . . what did he do? He shook her! He crushed her!

"He's choking me!" screamed Tecla, though she didn't really stop laughing. "Help! Help, somebody! He's gone crazy!"

Servants appeared. She was already so red she could no longer blush.

Thus they became engaged.

Then they got married. And for the honeymoon they chose San Godenzo, that quiet valley off the beaten track, with its comfortable small hotel sheltered from the road by a curtain of trees. His heart was so blissful that he almost forgot that it was somewhat sick; he went here and there, even climbed a few hillocks, with his still boyish, bouncing step; and the season was the one everyone had been expecting for years and he himself had hoped for since youth: an immortal summer.

Trebo scythes. Big bony Trebo, the peasant proprietor and shopkeeper, has locked up his general store, since there are almost no more vacationers, and has come to scythe his meadow for the last time. He wears long pants and a blue smock; his wife follows him dressed in light flowered cotton. He scythes, she rakes and gathers the hay in piles. Trebo scythes as though combing the meadow in a circle; the signs of it remain, equal, like those of a stone thrown in the water to make waves.

Filippi and his Tecla have climbed to the meadow to watch. This time I get up the courage to go there too.

Already it is late September. Early last night from my window I saw the diamond dust of the Pleiades, and even the daytime sky has a kind of moisture and softness of the starry sky. The cliffs are white with serenity, and nothing is far away. The sun has set where we are but still tinges the slope in front of us, and it seems not about to disappear; on one side that remaining field of rye sparkles like spring vetch; on the other that last unharvested wheat glows like phosphorus. Nothing is heard but the swish of the scythe.

The grass, once cut, changes color. It lies, enveloped in colorless shadings, on the bright green that remains, pale crests of an intense sea. And it exhales into the air an incense that I, already overflowing with happiness, can hardly bear.

Filippi, unobtrusively, puts his hand on his heart and, though standing still, pants.

"Lean harvest!" he says, if only to say something, aware that I'm observing him.

Especially incredible to the eye is the meadow saffron, or naked lady; it sprouts from the earth as bare flowers with no leaves. The flowers in some clearings are numerous: violet constellations in a sky of other worlds. Now they look like little hedge roses fallen where they lie; now they are amethysts. If you half close your eyes, they seem at times to be running, running, on Cinderella's little feet. When the scythe reaches them, they fall forward: eleven thousand martyred virgins.

"*Nackte Jungfern,*" says Tecla. "I wonder if that's what the Germans in this valley call them. Naked girls. Odd! I wonder why."

And she laughs without rhyme or reason; but no one, even if he didn't know her, would call her laugh silly. She laughs!

Standing near them, I can distinguish the shades of her perfume: in her hair, in her clothing, and mingled with her breath and her complexion. They rise, almost piercingly, the three shades, over the already unbearable odor of newly mown hay, itself so different from, and so similar to, the odor of must.

Filippi and I do not exchange looks. The woman is between us, and she makes both our hearts beat equally.

With the prongs of her rake, Trebo's wife separates

out the meadow saffron from the small piles of hay, for the cows don't like it. It is left behind, already flaccid and discolored.

Now I raise my eyes to Filippi's eyes, and they don't look right to me. I see them as wider and fixed. They stare at the light of the sun, which shifts from crag to crag; and they seem avid but mild, like eyes soon to close.

That's how I saw him, so to speak, for the last time.

But what am I saying? Was I dreaming? In a sunless meadow, opposite us and fairly distant, a woman remained, wearing a black skirt down to her heels as peasant women do in those parts. A woman dressed in black was wielding a scythe, and she looked too big.

"Valencia"

"Valencia": the best fox-trot.

I mean of the ones I know: I love dancing, especially the modern kind, but I don't know how to dance,
or don't dare, which comes to the same thing. Maybe
it's because I take everything too seriously, and it would
seem to me a responsibility, almost a sentimental commitment, to lead a woman, a beautiful unknown
woman, up and down, twirling her to the right and
twirling her to the left, while people are watching. And
it should also be said that I take things in an overly particular way; that when listening to dance music, I follow the rhythm in its inflections and pursue it in its
syncopations, so if I tried to imitate it with my feet, I
would risk being carried away by the music, mistaking
the tempo, and looking boorish to boot. In former
days I would have been afraid of stepping on a woman's
train, when dresses still had trains.

I don't dance, but I enjoy watching, without envy. Especially when the jazz band plays "Valencia." Right after the first beats, the drumsticks break up the melody like a crumbly substance from which spreads a slightly bitter odor, sort of delicate and at the same time barbaric. In the free space of the dance floor, between the orchestra and the leather armchairs, couples cling to each other and sway, their steps narrow and insistent, the women on their toes vibrant as blades on the floor. You look only at their feet, so much does the appearance of people dancing lose in attractiveness in comparison with so taut and flexible a pastime. Even the heads of the women are less attractive—no, they're not all beautiful—leaning with neither abandon nor restraint on the shoulders of the men, with the napes of their necks exposed, no longer shadowed by wispy curls. Their momentary secrets, murmured from lips to ear, are immediately lost, and their smiles are sudden and cold, like flashes of sunlight reflected by glass, or else set on their faces like a gentle idiocy.

The last time I spent a couple of weeks at the Strand Palace, I idled away countless hours, afternoon and evening, watching this spectacle. How strange when once in a while the orchestra tackles an old waltz! Most people try their best to dance it by walking, smiling with that good-natured satisfaction that a clumsy past deserves; but a plump, elderly gentleman with flying coattails is not ashamed of his passion for the last century; he skips, leaps, swoops, and goes into giddy raptures, carrying along his dear consort, as chubby as he is, buxom, yielding a little more than necessary to the rapture, the whirl of the dance. Yes, once again we see the famous gyrations of dance, or rather a single gyration: a double spinning top in a ballroom, a small cyclone imprisoned in a glass-paned hothouse. And the gyration makes us laugh. We can love only modern dancing, measured and ironic—a frenzy that, like the rest of our life, imitates reason.

Now the musicians have finished, and the dancers have returned to their tables. All you hear is the tinkle of cups and glasses and the dry dust cloud of conversation. But if you cock an ear, you can hear, at intervals beyond the big windows, the sighing of the sea, and the waltz tune has remained in the air. How ridiculous it was to see it danced! And how beautiful and sad to recall it! The music of today has a physical flavor, which may be pleasing at first but leaves no regrets. The last melancholy strains were those of the tango.

Days and days have passed, all of them the same. I've already had enough. And so has the woman who is keeping me company.

People have left, people have arrived, always the same. If they weren't so well brought up, they'd bite their nails out of boredom.

We are fed up with resting, tired of solitude in the midst of the crowd. We've become disgusted with these men and women without imagination, who do not enjoy the game of life except at the poker table and experience its tempo only in the tempo of the fox-trot.

As always happens to me in the fashionable world, a desert has formed around me. The desert of a large hotel, glaring lights, pearls, shirtfronts, pink shoulders, and yawns with gold teeth.

And yet, out of inertia, we're unable to tear ourselves away. It's already a feat that we manage to stand somewhat aloof. In these last days, instead of in the ballroom, we're in the lounge next to it, I reading a book, she doing beadwork, but all that separates us from the ballroom is a large square space, its sliding partition open, so that if you want to look, you have only to turn your head. And you hear whether you want to or not, as though you were right in the middle of it.

Today there's something new. My heart is full of sadness, and I'm choked up, for no reason, by a desire that has no goal, a feeling of guilt that has forgotten its origin. Shortly—it is four-thirty—the music will start. How will he dare to "entertain" me, that musician with his mournful mug, player of three cheerful instruments: the musical saw, the flexatone, the deafening whistle? I'll surely be unable to withstand it and will have to flee. The afternoon light in March is cutting, sharpened by the wind; and, for the first time since I'm here, the sea is angry and gnaws the rocks, leaving its foam behind. But you scarcely hear the roar in the closed lounge; you might as well be underground.

New too are the travelers sitting almost diagonally across from us, on the other side of the room, and gazing idly toward the ballroom. They arrived yesterday, mother and daughter, but have not yet been seen in society. I had a glimpse of the girl by herself this morning as, dressed in blue, with an enchanting step, she ascended the outside flight of steps on the side of the sea, which was all sprinkled with sunlight like a stairway to paradise.

Foreigners, certainly, from the North, but from what country? And, I would add, what time? They remind me of certain Meissen porcelain figurines; their oval faces have an eighteenth-century softness.

The mother is still flourishing—what a pity she doesn't wear a white wig above her high forehead. Two beautiful diamonds sparkle in her eyes. The daughter is a genuine blond, and instead of cutting her hair she has gathered it at the back of her neck so as to feign a modern style. And her dress too has been cut by a modern seamstress, as it should be, and yet how strange is that sky-blue velvet interspersed with bands of silver, colors of the full moon and the music of Mozart!

"There she is," my companion tells me in a low voice.

"Who? Which?"

"That one," she insists. And in a whisper, "The sick one."

Yes, I've been told that a girl who has recently arrived, the most beautiful girl in the hotel, is tubercular and beyond all hope. It's she all right, but you'd never know it. She has put on a little lipstick and rouged her cheeks but has spread it so nicely as to become all rosy, her face slightly reddened either by sudden modesty or some childish pleasure. And also, on her, the makeup is innocence; the lips, though tinted, remain chaste; the artifice and cosmetics are cleansed by the incredible look of those eyes: blue, pure, virginal, immense, so incredibly out of fashion that one would like to see them weep and to take pity on them so as to be able to believe once more in grief.

A hustle and bustle in the ballroom, the sound of footsteps on the orchestra platform—so it begins.

She half opens her mouth in an expression of candid curiosity; her eyes light up with a love in which there is no craving. She will not dance but with delight will watch other women dancing.

But three listless men leave the gaming table at the back of the room where we're sitting, move toward the partition, and take up the whole threshold in order to watch the dancing. She won't be able to see a thing. She opens her mouth a little more, wiggles her left forefinger slightly, and says, almost in a whisper, "Oh! . . . Oohh!"—a joking sort of lament, barely audible, and I alone have heard it—in the tone of a rather grown-up little girl from whom a plaything has been taken away in jest. And she is resigned and bows her chin on her breast, but her eyes still shine.

The three men have not noticed her. I get up to tell them, but now it's too late. Either by their own impulse or out of some sense of uneasiness that finally reaches them from that unheard sigh they move back and return to the table in the rear. Their looks graze the blond head without pausing. The view is clear.

She is full of gratitude.

Blissful and radiating bliss, she is wholly intent on the dance that has just begun.

Yes, "Valencia," the best fox-trot.

This is perhaps the only one, among the new dances known to me, that can be remembered with sadness, that leaves a furrow in the soul, like a caress that has made us tremble. Even as I hear it I relive it like a memory.

The drumsticks beat it out, giving rise to fragrant fumes, secret aromas of lands where I will never be, invitations to which I won't respond. The couples sway, almost motionless, suspended in the supple rhythm. A boy in short pants and his little sister dance all the way from one end of the ballroom to the other, happily and rapidly, as in a galop.

This piece has mutes and silences. It sounds like the music on board a ship that has weighed anchor and sailed away; and the wind now increases it, now extinguishes it.

The foreign girl is completely absorbed in contemplation with her large, radiant eyes. It is her solitary heart that dances. The rosy tint on her face has become a blush.

It is then that my eyes fill with tears, and I don't try to hide them.

"What's the matter?" says my lady friend. "What is it? Are you ill?"

"It's just," I say, taking advantage of a crescendo in the music, "that if by now I haven't learned to live, I never will. Look at her!" And I motion toward the foreign girl.

"Stop it!" she insists, irritated. "Don't make a spectacle of yourself. You might at least turn your head away."

She's right. I can at least turn my head. I glue my face to the window. The sea all of a sudden has become calm, more blue than the sky. I seem to see the ship sailing away. It sends forth music toward the shore, and from the shore the aromas of the gardens go forth to meet the music.

But I weep freely, foolish as a child, with my head in my hands and my shoulders shaken by sobs.

Sweet and base unhappiness to feel, finally, unhappy for someone else!

A crisis; now it's over. I can turn around again, dry my eyes, and show my face. It is just the moment when "Valencia" has ended. But the dancers, standing in the middle of the ballroom, clapping their hands a bit, are requesting an encore. It starts all over again. The drumsticks exult once more in their light jubilation.

The girl has had a little fit of coughing, exquisitely gracious, the only one I've heard in all this time. She has slowly turned her head on its lovely neck and for the first time has looked at me. Something in my disturbed expression, in my reddened eyes, has attracted her; she has stared at me, for a few moments, with compassionate eyes. Then she has leaned toward her mother and whispered some words in her ear.

But I've caught one of them: *unglücklich,* in a tone that could not deceive me. She has said I must be very unhappy if I'm not ashamed to weep in public, to show myself in public like this.

Once again she looks at me with distant benevolence. Then her eyes, newly illuminated, return to the dancing.

She is perfectly happy. *She* has had pity on me and would never have believed that I thought I was suffering for her.

In the serenity of her eyes, limpid as the sea now is, my wandering pain has shipwrecked in silence.

The Boy

"Cargo not proceeding to Messina. *Buona Fortuna* laid up for repairs in Genoa. Seriously damaged by storm. Will take three months."

He read the telegram half aloud, half paraphrasing it from memory. And when he brought it close to his eyes, he looked to see if it was transparent, as one does with banknotes to make sure they're not false.

"The *Buona Fortuna* they called it, that floating wreck, that old tub! 'Awaiting orders for perishable goods.' What orders?"

No one in the family dared breathe.

"Oh, Holy Virgin!" he resumed, striking the palms of his hands together. "Unless I go to Genoa and see it with my own eyes, I'll be the one who's ruined. Along with all the rest of you."

"You?" sighed his wife. "And how could you make the trip?"

For three days he had been in the armchair, with his gouty leg extended on a stool, so racked by pain that he didn't even dare to have himself put to bed. At one point it seemed to him that, by a miracle, necessity had cured him, and he unbandaged his knee, which looked shiny and enormous. His head drooped, but still he wanted to try, and supporting himself on the cane that he kept within reach, he put his foot on the floor and raised himself up. He fell back in the chair, with his mouth open like that of a tragic mask, full of silent moans. His trembling wife came running and resettled him on the couch.

"Consolata!" he called her after a while, in a tone of voice that the boy and the two little girls understood and immediately obeyed by filing out of the room.

"The boy," he asked, hesitating, when he was alone with his wife, "couldn't he go to Genoa? Would he be able to handle it?"

"That boy is pure gold," she replied.

Thus it was decided that Nicolangelo, who was nineteen and had never been out of Messina, Nicolangelo, who after the third year of technical high school had seen nothing outside his home except the gloom of the warehouse and the wharf in the harbor, would leave on this fabulous expedition. His little sisters, when they heard the great news, began to look up to him like a god. He was really pure gold, though of a pallid, olive complexion, with a big shock of very dark, rather curly, and lusterless hair; and in all his life he was unaware of having committed any other sin but smoking a few cigarettes in secret. That he was a handsome boy only his mother had told him, since he avoided other women. He called his mother *tu;* while, in accordance with the old custom, he deferred to his elderly father, who was old enough to be his grandfather, by kissing his hand and calling him Vossignoria.

To the minute instructions that his father kept giving him for the journey he answered only "Yes, Vossignoria," and "Don't worry, Vossignoria," or else responded more simply with an obsequious nod of his head. They dressed him in his dark, shabby Sunday suit, with the black bow tie; his father entrusted him with the requisite funds, ordering him to write down all his expenses to the last centesimo, and supplied him with long-winded letters of recommendation for the employees of the shipping company and customs office and for the proprietor of an inn where he himself had stayed fifteen years before; his mother gave him a few lire and a little picture of the Madonna della Lettera.

So Nicolangelo departed, seen off at the station by his weeping mother and sisters. His father had raised himself on his pillows so as to follow him with his eyes as far as possible, almost to the stair landing.

Night and day, between sleep and waking, the boy saw or glimpsed tunnels and mountains, beaches and the waves of the sea. His black canvas suitcase was secured with a chain and lock to the overhead rack in the compartment, for fear of thieves.

But in Genoa the owner of the Albergo del Pilota had no recollection of the traveler from Messina who had stayed in his establishment fifteen years before; and shaking his head and sticking out his lip, he perused the curious missive, written in solemn language like a letter of credit. "Lots of people go through here. Fifteen years is a long time," he said in conclusion, handing back the letter and indicating a room on the second floor, the only one in the whole place that by pure chance was free. Between the chilly reception and the unforeseen price of the lodging, the boy had the feeling of being alone and betrayed; his face darkened and he looked around with suspicion. Had they prepared some sort of trap for him? He had no wish for anything until evening came and stayed holed up in his room staring at his suitcase, hoping to get through it all the next day and depart immediately for Messina.

Then he went down to the dining room with no other thought but to study the price list carefully and choose the least expensive dish. The room was ordinary, poorly lit, and the tablecloths didn't all look clean. But that spring foreigners in Genoa were staying wherever they could, waiting for rooms to be available in this or that Riviera hotel, and at the next table Nicolangelo saw people of another race and clime: two tall, blond men, with broad, careless gestures and loud laughter, their shirtfronts white, and at each button-hole a pearl as big as a chickpea. Between them sat a woman, she too tall and blond, with her throat and shoulders naked or just barely covered by a loose, pale violet veil, like a mist on a beautiful mountain surrounded by sunlight, marvelous to behold, a divine being, a queen, whom he could almost touch with his hand. They were certainly rich, "millionaires," "Americans," bursting with health and joy. They were laughing, no doubt, at the adventurous necessity that had forced them to take shelter for the night in this fleabag hotel and the whim that had prompted them to eat fried fish in this dump of a restaurant. Having finished the fish, they peeled bananas and sliced the pineapple they had brought from outside wrapped in tissue paper; they poured champagne and laughed, their laughter alternating with chatter and strange and delightful warblings.

The boy hadn't the least idea what they had in mind or what their words meant. All he could see was that the woman kept staring at him every minute. Why? Was he so poor and ridiculous? Did she perhaps want to give him something out of charity, a few coins to help him pay for his supper and not look like a spendthrift in his father's eyes? Disturbed, he went upstairs to his room and in the lamplight stared straight at his face, and at both profiles, in the wardrobe mirror; he retied his necktie and yanked at the hem of his jacket to adjust it to his waist. Suddenly a thought, so tumultuous as to overwhelm him, crossed his mind: Was he really a "handsome boy," as his mother said; were his well-shaped nose, olive pallor, velvety eyes, and heavy, curly head of hair such as statues have pleasing to this divine woman; did she love him? Almost without feeling the blood in his veins, he returned to the dining room, and the look he encountered on the threshold, from under golden eyelashes, was a serious and passionate one. The woman, unobserved by her companions, raised her glass and drank to him. Once he was seated, they rose to leave, but she, lingering behind, passed alongside him and said something over his head, a word as elusive and fragrant as a white blossom falling from a flowering tree.

Then he shut himself up in his room, without

bolting the door, and lay in wait, his heart in his throat. It was after midnight when in the hallway he heard footsteps, which he recognized. Doors closed, sounds died away. Looking out, he saw that the woman was waiting for him in the doorway of her room, and only her eyes signaled to him. He was unable to keep from whispering, as he approached her, "Vossignoria called me?" But she hushed him and drew him inside.

There were moments in those hours when he wanted to cry out. She closed his mouth with her hand, which gave off a perfume stronger than incense.

Twice he asked her name: "*Come ti chiami?*" She shook her head and laughed. And hearing her laugh, he would have liked to kill her.

When it was time to leave, he felt himself the master and said to her firmly, "*Domani.*" She repeated laboriously, "*Do-ma-ni?*" and, holding him back a moment longer, went to look it up in a red pocket dictionary. "*Niente do-ma-ni,* no tomorrow," she said, having figured it out and, stroking his hair, pushed him gently out of the room.

The boy did not sleep. At the first light of dawn he carefully got dressed, and even before the front door of the hotel was open he had sat down to wait in the narrow vestibule, in a wicker chair beside the desk clerk's counter, while the porter was sweeping the floor. They kept looking at him suspiciously. But he thought nothing of it and waited for hours.

No sooner did the woman appear, so light and serene you would have said she had invisible wings, than he stood up to confront her. She, unfazed, turned her head aside and moved toward the exit. He blocked her path. Whereupon the woman, blushing, turned on her heel and went back up the stairs. It was some time before she reappeared, between her companions. They looked like her; they were surely her brothers.

Nicolangelo again got up and stepped forward, prepared to speak. The three were only briefly disconcerted, and one of the two men, leaving the woman a little behind as though under the protection of the other, said curtly, in English, "Get out of the way!" Having said this, he rejoined the others so that they occupied the whole width of the vestibule. They went out on the street.

He stood there without moving, his feet rooted to the spot and his whole body quivering. But his voice didn't tremble when he asked the proprietor, who had witnessed the scene from a corner, "Who are those people? What are their names?"

"Your room," replied the hotelkeeper, "is taken. You are asked to check out before noon."

Then he too went out and almost like a sleepwalker went looking for a gun dealer's shop. Had someone asked him what he intended to do, he might have replied, awakening with a start from this daze, that he'd decided to kill himself. Later he recalled having hesitated a long time over the choice of the revolver, because he wanted something good but cheap and felt he had to write down how much it cost in the little account ledger given him by his father.

The gun in his pocket, he went back to the hotel and walked up and down in the sunlight on the sidewalk outside. When the trio came back, he ran and planted himself in their path.

"The young lady is my bride."

And he spoke these absurd words with an absurd gesture of his right hand, as though presenting a bouquet of flowers. He even managed to touch the woman's hand, but she drew back.

"Get the hell out of here, you idiot!" said one of the two men, in English. And, turning to the proprietor and the desk clerk: "Throw the son of a bitch out!"

The desk clerk was the first to grab the boy from behind. But he jumped back and, whipping out the gun, said "Your sister is a . . ." and fired at her pointblank.

The jury acquitted him. It would have been no better or worse for him had they sent him to prison for a number of years. His father died of a heart attack during the trial. Now everyone in Messina can see him, the poor boy who a few years ago was "pure gold," when during the long summer twilights he stands in the doorway of the dark warehouse to take the fresh air. He is as thin as he used to be and dressed in black, and his antique pallor is still as pleasing to women tourists and seems to them fatal. Only a little premature gray mars his dense head of hair, and he is even more silent than before; he has nothing to say to anyone.

Hands

Although she is quite young, not yet twenty-four, a vein in her hand already stands out prominently, the one that descends from the forefinger toward the thumb and loses its way in the hollow that corresponds on the back of the hand to the mount of Venus, as the palmists call it. On closer examination, one finds others, especially in the thin wrist on the side of the palm; but the one I'm talking about is the one one notices first, where more blood flows, red blood within a blue sheath. Ever since we've been in love, I've traced this vein on her skin several times with my fingernail without hurting her, or I've marked it with a trail of tiny kisses, saying, "Here is Basilia's little blue stream, hidden amid little golden ferns." I say this to her without embarrassment, because I've discovered (or rediscovered once again in my life) that one goes on saying the same silly things when love returns.

It's a mystery to me how on this hand—which is not tiny, a doll's hand, but neither is it large—aspects of youth, or rather of adolescence, coexist with aspects that are not of youth or anything else, but steady ones, resembling a destiny. The hollow is tender, pinkish white, of a shade so new that it seems washed now and then in the waters of earthly paradise; so naked that it seems to blush a little from its very nakedness; and when I look at it, it seems incredible to me that I've kissed her, this woman. But the other side of the hand, the one always exposed to one's gaze and to the light, belongs to another creature, olive skinned, tenacious, or, when the light is reflected in a certain way, filled with dark golden specks. Burnt pink—that's the only way I can put it—under the fingernails, aromas pressed and enclosed under five little caps of onyx! Pensive vein! The complicated, inextricable knots of the phalanges, like Leonardesque knots, like your obstinacy and your silences, Basilia! And the wrist is so fragile that often, if I close my eyes, I have no choice but to picture it cut, bleeding.

She had looked at me many times, so many times, in so many months! Later, when there was everything between us, she said to me—in the subdued voice with which she speaks of herself—that "everything had been decided" from the first time she'd seen me. But how could I have been aware of it then? How could I have interpreted it that way? So young, little more than an adolescent, with a baby girl a few months old, whom I had not seen (and was never to see) and who must have been like a new doll for her! So taciturn and reserved! The husband, tall and pale, stood behind her chair in the evenings, a few steps away; he didn't let her out of his sight; his gaze, filtered through his long blond eye-lashes, made him look even paler, and he seemed to be weaving a fabric of invisibility and spreading it across his wife's bare shoulders so that no one would see them.

Her gaze rested on me, and she had no fear. It was as though she knew nothing of danger or evil; I don't know what she was looking for in my eyes; thus it sometimes happens that a little bird, coming in the window, starts poking about the middle of the room with no fear that someone might catch it. Really, her eyes were modest in color: like nightingale feathers or the wings of sparrows. They were tenacious but bland. I let her gaze wander, not daring to intercept it, and I still didn't realize that this was for fear that, had I tried to do so, she would get frightened and fly away.

I thought I was convinced that this woman had no importance; her name, Basilia, sounded oddly excessive to me. In society she was a wallflower, with little to say; it was also rare to see her smile.

One evening—we found ourselves by chance seated next to each other on a settee, far from the others in the music room—that evening she slowly slipped off her right glove before my eyes, and for the first time my eyes discovered the physiognomy of her hand. Then I felt a real tumult in my heart, a strong throb. I almost feared that she, seated beside me, would hear it. With my hand I clutched the fabric on which I was sitting so as not to clutch at her.

Thus everything was decided.

The whole story of our love was really without words until the end.

Looking into each other's eyes, seeking each other, fleeing each other, we learned from one day to the next a rare and precious language that no one will ever know as we knew it. All the things that count in our lives, the splendid things and the sad ones, happened and will happen in silence.

A large part of our story lay in my wish to make a prisoner of her hand, and in resisting this temptation, and in the fear of spoiling everything.

Other eyes preferred her shoulders, round and soft like those of Psyche; other eyes, unrestrained, sought her knees in their pink organzine stockings. Not I. The long vigil of our terrible sin was as pure—if one can use this word—as a wedding vigil ought to be.

I felt I was only attracted by what anyone could have—by the hand that many men could kiss, the fingers that many could hold in theirs while greeting her. But they didn't know what they were kissing, what they were holding. To me her five fingers seemed like prodigious flowers, unique orchids in the depths of some shadowy forest, distant water lilies on waters of perdition; and I didn't know when the day would come for me to pick them. Her right hand wore only one ring, a ruby, where you would have said that all the blood in that hand was collected; the other was entirely bare. It's strange how seldom I happened to look at the two of them together. Then the left hand seemed to have no independent existence but was the image of the other mirrored by the air; and it was incredible that the mirror of the air did not also reflect that shining clot of blood.

How many precautions so as not to touch it with the light touch that reveals love! If I was obliged to press her hand, I did so almost brusquely, as is done between men; if I had to kiss it, I waited until it was inside a glove. Once a small handkerchief of hers fell at my feet; I retrieved it and handed it back to her from as far away as I could, even taking care not to graze her fingertips. I was afraid I'd cry out if I touched her. One evening as I opened the door of an automobile for her, our hands almost met on the handle. I retracted mine, afraid she would murmur to me conventionally "Oh, excuse me!"—and that everything would be over for good. On the lake we kept the tempo in rowing, I facing her; her cousin at the rudder. The motion of the oars carried us in turn to melodious distances, to proximities that until the last moment seemed unavoidable; the tranquil waters danced a vertigo in which I sank.

I felt the vertigo in the box of the theater where sometimes we met. Her plump arms, when she took off her cape, smelled sweet; the vaccination scars on her tawny arms were like seals on the crust of warm, fragrant bread. Slowly she removed her gloves, and it took so much time! The glove abandoned beside her remained inflated by the lovely form that was no longer there. Now her hand lay on the velvet parapet, and it was as though it were all of her, Basilia suddenly uncovered.

Later it was a chill—and a flare-up—when my hand finally descended on hers. It was such a long September afternoon, with such unmoving clouds in the sky, that you might think nothing more would ever happen, anywhere.

All of a sudden a magnolia leaf drifted down from

its tree and landed on the gravel. I can't say it fell. It descended so slowly that everything all around it seemed to be watching.

We were alone, Basilia and I, on the broad empty terrace of her villa by the lake. She was seated near a stone balustrade, leaning on the parapet with its scant green moss and looking out. I was standing behind her chair in the same position in which I had often seen her husband; and when I realized it I had a strange feeling that I was no longer myself.

The magnolia leaf had already lain for a few minutes on the ground. From the foliage of the same tree a bird started singing. Then as though clouds and water had been awakened, how painfully I can't say, time once again began to flow.

She turned her head to me; raised her face to me, her face, tortured as I had never seen it. But not even then did she say a word. Her hand, ringless, lay on the parapet.

I covered it with mine. How long the moments were before touching it! Each was precisely like the tolling of a bell.

With the same pressure of my fingers I felt the velvety warmth of her skin, the downy warmth, and the dryness of her tendons, the fluttering dryness of a captured butterfly.

O beloved, there was to be so much between us that was bad, along with so much that was good! People today know how to seize joy without effort; they have only to reach out; and we've had to bleed from a thousand thorns. Your little girl, whom I never saw, you never saw her again; your house is closed.

Every approaching day conceals a menace, and night often falls with remorse.

But I still cannot revive the time when we had a tomorrow—when you were not mine. Gazing steadily at your covered hand, with an entreaty in the language of silence that at that time you had already learned to understand, I sometimes ask you to take off a glove. You do so and barely smile.

Then I seize your hand, I snatch it like forbidden fruit. Long in mine do I clasp it, this image of you: this tawny hand of yours, serious like your face, throbbing like your heart.

The Mirage

We set out long before dawn with the stars and the black sky above us. Our headlights illuminated the spines of a thicket of prickly pear, which we immediately left behind, and the engine roared as we shifted into gear.

"Maybe," Annalìa said unexpectedly, "that's the only roar we'll hear for the whole trip."

"Of course," her husband agreed, without smiling and without raising his voice. And a while later, when I'd already forgotten what prompted the remark: "We won't even run across Tartarin's lion."

We were driving at an even speed on the caravan route, which was spattered by our light. We had figured carefully that, even going slowly, we should reach Bumunach not more than an hour or two after midday. We were stocked with maps, a compass, other instruments, and foodstuffs and beverages to last for a trip at least three times as long (this had made us smile when packing the bottles, thermoses, and canned food in the trunk, which we then secured behind the car), not counting a shopping bag full of cheap gifts destined for the inhabitants of the oasis where Annalìa had it in mind to acquire some white burnooses and necklaces or carved beads famous throughout the region.

Annalìa's words were still hanging in the air, and the roar of the motor brought them back to mind.

"A woman's voice on the threshold of the desert has an extraordinarily fresh sound. Like a fountain. It makes you thirsty."

I said this without sarcasm, and the husband, alluding to the thirst-quenching items we were carrying, remarked without irony, "We're well supplied."

But is there any need to explain that whatever was said and thought among the three of us was with neither irony nor sarcasm? Our relations, hard as it is to acknowledge states of mind so vibrant and fragile, were of a kind perhaps less rare than is generally thought. Corrado and I, inseparable friends, had met Annalìa on the same day, and we had talked about her between ourselves, as about many other persons and things, for months and months; but from one day to the next we had talked a little more about her and a little less about all the rest, carried away, without quite noticing it, by an admiration that grew to idolatry for a physical beauty and a spiritual grace the likes of which we'd never known. What marked the difference between Corrado and me, though it did nothing to separate us, was that all of a sudden he realized before I did that such idolatry was love, and when he told her so she became his wife. Annalìa, perhaps, until that moment had loved us both, without distinguishing too clearly between us, and in my heart of hearts I was never able to suppress the notion that she, with the same candor, would have accepted my hand had I been the first to give a name and purpose to the delightful sentiment that united the three of us to the detriment of none.

A situation of this kind ought to lead to the end of the friendship or to something deceitful and repugnant. But for us it was not like that, and I insist on believing that men and women are capable of living a beautiful life more often than they dare admit. We dared to say "we three" openly, without paying any attention to the gossip that the fact of our being a trio must have aroused. Even that night we felt the strange need to be "we three," the three of us alone in the desert, by leaving the mechanic at Rahal-Hamud and escaping the group that had come with us from Europe.

As others strain to achieve elegance of movement or muscular precision in sports, so we trained ourselves during the first year of Annalìa's marriage—Corrado to resist the inclination to jealousy, I to repress any thought that was not strictly fraternal. We succeeded almost easily, and as compensation we gained a way of experiencing life, a way, I would say, of breathing purely and grandly, as though only the air of dawn entered our lungs. For her part, Annalìa did not visibly demonstrate that she had any difficulties to overcome; and I always had the impression that, in a different way, we were both indispensable to her. I would have said, using an antiquated language that sounds ridiculous today, that for her Corrado was the reality and I the ideal.

We addressed one another with the familiar *tu*.

"You live always for tomorrow," she said to me, "for what is far away. Your mind is full of big, impossible things."

The truth is I almost never recognize people coming toward me on the street, and my eyes look beyond everyone in search of the horizon.

Since none of us had brothers or sisters, we considered siblinghood a sort of paradise, something good that had been promised and lost. We lived as though I were a brother of both Corrado and his wife. Neither of them minded if I rapidly drew my hand across her eyes, saying jokingly, "Open your eyes—I don't believe it."

It was indeed unbelievable that her eyes, in so dark complexioned a face, should be so green: green as malachite, with the pupil very narrow and unfathomable, like a tiny hole drilled in a gem by a diamond needle.

She opened them, laughing. Thus she showed her gums—her sole defect, but it gave charm to a beauty that otherwise would have been too perfect—and her thin lips seemed to swell, and her mouth resembled a carnation.

That was how I saw her eyes and her smile that morning as the light of dawn spread across the desert. The car stopped.

"There," said Annalìa, turning toward me but without pointing to the landscape, "that's what we've been dreaming of."

The undulating solitude was a vision. The light, which at the horizon had the color of an iris, on the earth was a basin of roses. The brightness shrunk the distances, and it seemed to live in a large globe of motionless crystal.

"Now we're happy," I said. "We weren't happy when we started out."

Often we had the same feelings without communicating them. In the night, at the moment of departure, and just before the motor began to roar, we had suffered from the sort of anxiety you feel when on your way to meet a destiny.

"Now," I added, laughing, "we'll have hallucinations of hearing and vision. We'll hear the desert drum. We'll see mirages."

"Mirages!" Annalìa exclaimed to me. "The big, impossible things. Tomorrow!"

Other times she had spoken these words to me, or almost the same ones. But I had been able to banish the suspicion that she was trying, in a tone between regret and irony, to suggest that my nature was as trusting in the future as it was perplexed and incapable of seizing on the present; that she almost meant to reproach me for having been unable to forestall Corrado and love her for myself. Now this thought, which I found odious, caught me by surprise there on our morning stop, and I was disturbed by it.

We had breakfast without dipping into our real

provisions, serving ourselves from a wicker basket that we had set aside; then we started out again. Annalìa was at the wheel and, turning around, said "Good-bye! Good-bye!" in a tone more pathetic than playful, as though she were bidding a last farewell to invisible Rahal-Hamud, the inhabited world, the past, and everything.

"Why did you say that?" Corrado asked her with a certain harshness. "Maybe it would be better to turn back!" But she didn't answer.

We knew the direction; we knew that the caravan route was frequented daily, and two days earlier we had explored some twenty kilometers of it so as not to miss a certain fork in the road that we had heard about. We were not really the first to cross (and for such a short stretch!) the desert by automobile, and none of us was fearful by nature. And yet each felt the anxiety of the other two, like a bundle of nearby vibrations.

The air soon became scorching, and the sultriness seemed to decompose bodies and souls. The saline gray glitter of the stony ground was so dizzying that one sometimes had the impression of proceeding amid little eddies of quicksilver. Suddenly we had to confront a stony slope, of which we had not been warned, and we were no longer sure of the road, but looking back and mirroring ourselves in our own pale and troubled faces, we judged it impossible to turn around. When the car, striking a bump that had escaped Corrado's attention (for some time he had replaced his wife at the wheel), bounced like a bucking horse, we felt a sense of liberation, because by now the mental tension, in expectation of an evil that seemed to us imminent and certain, had become unbearable.

We immediately heard a thud and then more rapid ones. The trunk, insecurely fastened and dislodged by the shocks, was rolling down the slope. We found it at the bottom, half smashed; many bottles of mineral water, champagne, and other beverages had been broken, and the tepid, dirty mixture had spoiled the foodstuffs. We economically saved whatever we could, choked by an imaginary torment of thirst, and panting carried the trunk back up the slope. Annalìa, pale in her helmet, was waiting for us. Since the car had not suffered serious damage, we were able to continue on our way. The trunk, now half empty, accompanied every jolt with a dreadful clanking of tin cans.

All traces of a road had disappeared. Violent plumes of sulfur hung in the sky. All of a sudden I half raised myself and, pointing to the horizon, exclaimed, "There!"

White minarets, dark gardens, Moorish palaces with windows filled with a light as fresh as beatitude, and lines of motionless camels at the edge of the shade unfolded before our eyes. Annalìa's profile, in contemplation, was angelic. We knew that the little oasis of Bumunach contained no such marvels and were not deceived by the vision. But whoever has not seen a mirage cannot understand the fearful joy it gives for a few minutes.

We lowered our eyes and kept going. About an hour may have passed when Annalìa, with a start, asked, "Aren't those the bells of the Christian church at Rahal-Hamud?"

"Don't say it! Don't say such damn fool things!" shouted her husband. "It's impossible to hear the bells of the Christian church at Rahal-Hamud."

Toward evening there was another apparition. We saw a kiosk of lapis lazuli and gold, more beautiful than the mosque of Omar. But none of us said a word. When night fell we got out of the car.

The stars shone. For a long time we didn't speak. Then Annalìa, without looking at the stars, said, "There must be something divine . . . something inconceivable . . . in this life or in another."

After a pause, she asked, "What does 'Bumunach' mean?"

"'Munach,'" I replied, knowing a few words of Arabic, "is the place where the camels kneel."

Then we said nothing more.

We slept for a long time. The pitiless sun awoke us, stinging our eyes. We had no hope of salvation unless someone, or a miracle, were to come along.

At noon the tempestuous wind rose, blowing waves of sand and fire over us. But through the sand I saw a spot, the spot of the oasis, like a dark cloud beyond a lighter one and, stretching out my arm, I shouted, "There it is!"

"No! No!" cried Corrado angrily. And Annalìa, closing her eyes, said, "The third mirage. And the last."

The car wouldn't budge, and it was being covered by sand.

"This way! Come with me!" I cried with whatever strength of mind I had left. But I could not persuade them, and Corrado held his wife back with his hand.

Perhaps it was because I had believed in the mirage that I was able to reach it. Bending low, practically crawling, I got away from the area of the sandstorm, and after walking for six hours, almost out of my mind with terror and fatigue, I reached Bumunach. The shadows of the palm trees merged with the shades of evening, and close to the well I saw the sparkling eyes, silent and dark, of women; Annalìa's green eyes were surely closed forever. The chieftain of the oasis offered me refreshment and coffee black as night.

I told him what had happened. He said only, "You lost your way. Rahal-Hamud is not far."

I had no tears. I asked him for a caravan to look for my dear companions at dawn and, if possible, transport their bodies home.

"Whatever is necessary must be done," he replied. "This is necessary."

About the Author

Giuseppe Antonio Borgese was born in Polizzi Generosa, Sicily, in 1882. By the age of twenty-seven he was one of Italy's foremost literary critics and the founder of two literary journals. He became the chair of the German literature department at the University of Rome in 1909 but was forced into exile when he refused to take the oath of allegiance to Mussolini—one of only twelve Italian university professors to do so. He lived in the United States from 1931 until 1947. Borgese's many works include the novel *Rubè* and the anti-Fascist essay *Goliath: The March of Fascism.* He died in Fiesole in 1952.